Johnny Voodoo

Johnny Voodoo

by Dakota Lane

DELACORTE PRESS

Published by
Delacorte Press
Bantam Doubleday Dell Publishing Group, Inc.
1540 Broadway
New York, New York 10036

Library of Congress Cataloging-in-Publication Data
Lane, Dakota.
    Johnny Voodoo / Dakota Lane.
      p. cm.
    Summary: When her father moves her and her younger brother from Manhattan to Louisiana after the death of her mother, fifteen-year-old Deirdre is desolate until she meets a strange young man known as Johnny Voodoo, who helps her learn about love.
    ISBN 0-385-32230-5 (alk. paper)
    [1. Grief—Fiction. 2. Love—Fiction. 3. Family problems—Fiction. 4. Louisiana—Fiction.] I. Title.
PZ7.L231785Jo 1996
[Fic]—dc20   95-53830
                                                CIP
                                              AC

The text of this book is set in 12.5-point Adobe Garamond.

Book design by Julie E. Baker

Manufactured in the United States of America

November 1996

10 9 8 7 6 5 4 3 2 1

BVG

To Zhenya, Benita, Alex, and Hailey
and thanks to Jewel

Chapter 1

I'm suffering from severe culture shock. I hate my father's guts. And I'm in love with a homeless person. It's not as bad as it sounds; or maybe it's worse. Maybe I'm so crazy I'm actually strapped into a mental-hospital bed, and I just *think* I'm walking home from school, down these soggy Louisiana streets.

I have bizarre thoughts like that all the time, although I try not to think of anything having to do with hospitals. I hardly went to see Mom when she was in one. She was there for three months. And then took off. It's easier to think of it that way. I never think of the hospital or her body. I just imagine her zipping around having a blast somewhere up in the stratosphere. Or maybe in some beautiful new baby's body. Mom believed in reincarnation.

I don't know what I believe anymore, except I'm not thrilled with God. Just the word *God* is a big blank to me. When I see it in a book, I skip over that part. And I don't believe in prayers or meditation anymore. Maybe there is something out there, but probably not. Still, I remember the way Mom would look so happy and calm when she did her meditations in that little room off her bedroom with the sun coming in the window and the dried flowers in the little blue vase.

Man, I miss that girl. She always called me girl. Hi, girl! Hey, girl! What's happening, girl! And I called her girl right back. We were like sisters. Oh, that sounds so corny, it's ridiculous. But we were. She had me when she was seventeen. And my father, Curtis the creep, was such a jerk that my mom basically took care of me all by herself. She was a real good mom. Great cook. Sewed stuff. Really listened when I talked. Hardly yelled at me and my brother, Kenny. She smelled like vanilla and rain. She wound fresh sunflowers into the ribbons of the last birthday presents she gave me. Don't get me started.

If she were here I might be able to stand this place. I don't want to get all weird and religious, but maybe she is here. Sometimes I feel her. I can just hear what she'd say right this second: "Oh, Dee, look at that guy there with the kittens on him!"

I walk down these strange, dripping, green streets underneath the low, white sky and get the creeps looking at things. Like that big black guy sitting on his porch with all those newborn kittens crawling up and down his big shirt. He looks almost sinister to me. And then I hear my ma. "Oh, Dee, check that out!" And this little laugh of delight. If she were here, she'd give the guy a wink or something and he'd break into a big smile. It'd be a great, human, warm moment.

Only she's not here. That brief feeling of her being here is gone and it's just me standing on the glittery sidewalk looking at the guy with the kittens. And I'm not the type to wink.

Sometimes I can hardly even smile. Sometimes my body feels so weird and I feel so self-conscious I can hardly make my legs and arms move and get down the street in a normal way.

The terrible moment's over and there's this huge rush of relief—I'm past his house! Then I have to deal with the next set of people on their porches.

My house is three miles from school, on Princessa Street, a one-block dead-end road that runs down a hill straight into the bayou, which is like an overgrown swamp. It takes almost an hour to get home from school. To make the time pass, sometimes I pretend I'm back home in Manhattan, walking down Fifth Avenue. It takes a lot of concentration, but as I walk past the small, faded candy-colored houses, I pretend I'm passing skyscrapers and familiar landmarks, like my favorite bookstores, my old savings bank, the Italian shoe store, the loft where Marissa lives with her mom on the top floor.

I keep doing this until I've imagined going down twenty city blocks. And when I see that old guy selling sweet potatoes and sugarcane on the corner of Margerita and Olive, I just pretend it's the pretzel man on the corner of Fifth and Twentieth. I don't think there's one place in all of Charmette, Louisiana, where you can buy a big, salty pretzel with hot mustard on top. Those New York pretzels were crunchy and golden on the outside, soft and doughy on the inside. Nothing can keep a crunch in Louisiana except for pork rinds, and I don't eat pigs.

I end the Charmette–turns–New York game when I turn onto Olive Street, a wide, tree-lined boulevard that runs alongside New Day Park.

Since last Tuesday, I walk slowly when I pass the park, even when the kids inside stare out the green gates at me and make me feel like running.

I met the homeless person there last Tuesday morning when I was walking to school.

I didn't know he was a homeless person at the time. He looked about seventeen. He had a beautiful face. Correction. He had the most beautiful face I'd ever seen. His eyes were so dark they were almost black. He had long, dark brown hair to his shoulders. He wore a black hat. He was mysterious and sweet. I could tell he was brilliant even though he just said a few things to me in his quiet voice. He had an incredible smile. His eyes sparkled.

"Hello" was all he said as I walked past the park last Tuesday. I almost jumped fifty feet. He was standing with his face stuck between the spokes and his arms wrapped around them like he was a prisoner. My first thoughts were of sick things. Kidnapping. Mugging. I saw a quick flash of silver and I thought, *knife*. Then I saw it was the silver fold in an old-fashioned accordion hanging over his shoulder on a strap.

In the city you never talked to strangers. Not even cute strangers, because you never stopped long enough to see if they were cute or to notice that the knife was really an accordion. I was losing my city edge. So I kept on walking.

"Where're you going in such a hurry?" he said. His voice was slidey and deep with a Louisiana accent. It wrapped itself around my brain and made me want to slow down.

I took a look back at him and the fear left me. After all, this was Charmette. It was a warm, hazy morning with birds calling in the trees. Plenty of cars were passing by. And his face was so open and friendly.

"I'm going to school," I said. I took a few steps

toward him. He nodded. I took a few more. "Hey, how come you aren't in school?"

He was silent for so long, I thought maybe I shouldn't have asked. Then he said, "I already know everything about the Louisiana Purchase that I ever need to know."

I thought that was funny, because we were just learning about the Louisiana Purchase in school. I got the feeling that this guy was kind of psychic. And then he proved it.

Standing there, I wished I were free like him and could hang around and skip school. As the cars rushed by with people on their way to work and school, I flashed that all of us were stuck on little tracks, coming and going from places we didn't want to be, sealed up inside our cars and classrooms like vampires in tombs.

I felt almost dizzy with the realization; it made everything look different. Even the park seemed different—a little parcel of earth encased behind bars, shut off from the cement roads. A place where humans could pretend to have fun when they were done being sealed up in the things they hated.

And that's when he said, "We all make our own jails."

Just soft and casual, as if he'd been sharing my brain for a second and knew everything I was feeling and going through.

I wondered what his name was, and he stuck his arm out toward me and said, "My name's Johnny."

His hand was warm, and he held mine for just a second and then we both let go.

"Deirdre," I said. It was as if I'd had a spell cast over me. Or had one removed—one that made me clumsy and self-conscious and tied my tongue in knots.

"Deirdre." He said my name as if he were tasting it. There was something so innocent about him that he would've seemed a little ridiculous if the innocence hadn't been all mixed up with a kind of darkness. He acted as if it was a completely new experience for him just to be standing out there in the morning with the bars between us, saying my name.

"Deah-drah," he said. "It's a pleasure to meet you."

The sun broke through the sticky bank of clouds, and Johnny's dark hair was shot through with red lights.

He looked at me as if he'd be lost if I left. It would've been weird if any other stranger had looked at me that way, but Johnny was different.

If I didn't tear myself away, I'd miss the morning bell at school.

"Bye! I'll be late." I took off in a full run.

That day I found out more about Johnny than I

ever wanted to know. The worst thing was, I didn't know what parts were true and what parts were lies.

Apparently this demented girl, Liz Haddonfield, saw me hanging out with Johnny. And apparently she ran and told the entire tenth grade.

If it had been any guy, nobody would've cared. Ditto if I had been any girl. But I'm the weird girl from New York. And Johnny—well, they call him Johnny Voodoo.

This is Charmette High at noon: A bell splits the air. You push through the crowds and into the great hall, where the land of Cliqueville begins. Geek girls count their nickels and dimes for the cafeteria food. Heads and stoners check their linty pockets for stashed lunchtime joints. You go past the bathrooms, where the pseudopunks and glitter crowd stash their spray-paint cans to do a little decorating of the old brick walls outside the school—lyrics from the songs of their fave bands. I did all that back in seventh grade.

When I first walked into this school seven weeks ago, it was like the mid-eighties all over again. At first I thought maybe the kids were so cool they were out, onto the next thing, which was usually the past. But we'd already gone through our eighties revival in the city. And after that, we did the seventies.

8

When I walked into Charmette High, I figured I'd missed something. I mean, I was out of everything while Mom was dying.

There were always new little cults and trends popping up in the city, and most of the time I didn't pay too much attention. When Mom was sick I didn't care at all. Actually, it made me physically ill to see the new looks and hear the kids talking about the new stuff. Somewhere around the time the hip-hop girls turned into Kewpie Klones and the Grunge Girls gave up body-piercing for tattoos, and the boys were moving on from eyeliner to lipstick, and the raves became skating rinks, I just shut down and couldn't take any of it in anymore.

My best friend, Marissa, was in danger of becoming a Kewpie Klone when I left the city. I hadn't even noticed until a few days after Mom's funeral when Marissa came by and we went out to sit on my fire escape. She was wearing silvery pink lipstick and totally glam-girl eyes and a short cotton flower-print dress that looked as if it might have belonged to a five-year-old, and over that a long skirt made of fishnet and a big gray granny jacket with huge shoulder pads, and on the thin lapel of the jacket was this wild pin, space-age but like the fifties, with a little rocket ship turning around inside the circle of a moon, the pin actually moving as you looked at it.

And Marissa was saying things like "We found

this place last night, used to be a homeless shelter, and it was so down-low only three kids showed at first." Total Kewpie-speak. Kewpie was this skinny thrift-store underground type who'd been in a couple of videos and a couple of okay movies.

Seeing Marissa like that was like turning on the news in the middle of some kind of hostage crisis or world war that everybody knows about except you. Soon after that, I left town. I haven't talked to her or written her once. She doesn't have my address, as far as I know. One of these days I just might send Marissa a note. But everything I'm going through is too weird for words.

Like Charmette High at noon.

They've got these Southern groups and cliques you've never even heard of. I don't know if they call themselves these names or if the kids outside the cliques make up the names, but I hear stuff like "Yo, rockabilly," and "Watch out you don't get bent by no swampheads," and "He got burned by that marsh dog."

Then, over by the lockers, you hear the screaming white assholes. There are SWAs in New York, too, and everywhere, I guess. They're always boys. Usually big boys. They shove each other and get suddenly violent and slam their fists and feet into things that are sure to make a loud noise. They have big throats and curse a lot. Everything's a freak-out, whether they're happy or messed up.

You can see SWAs in the making as early as fourth or fifth grade, and by the time they hit high school they're full-blown. Within the SWA group there are SWA jocks and SWA lowlifes. There's not much difference between them except that the jocks go for sports and the lowlifes go for drinking. Both groups hate each other.

Usually you hear them before you see them; their noise gives you a big shot of adrenaline and you either want to run or kill somebody.

That Tuesday morning, the Morning of Meeting the Homeless Person, the SWAs were slamming around their lockers. I slid past them as usual, only I ran right into an SWA girlfriend (or SWAG), Claire Wright, best friend of the big-mouthed Liz Haddonfield. Like half the SWAGs, she had big breasts, a tight T-shirt, perfectly moussed hair (hers was dyed black), expertly applied pale pink lipstick, and an attitude as big as her chest.

A big chest meant a whole other thing in the city. The cool girls liked to slink around with their pale faces and shirts over shirts. They wore low-cut, see-through stuff only if they were flat. Big chests had to be covered or hidden. Tits weren't status symbols. Here it's totally retro.

"Say, Yankee," Wright said to me. "Say, Yankee Voodoo."

I knew they called me Yankee behind my back, but this was the first time someone had said it to my face.

Claire's boyfriend, tall and red-faced, with a red neck coming out of his buzz-cut head, was standing nearby. He started to sing in a hoarse voice, "Yankee Voodoo went to town, riding on a Johnny. . . ."

That was my first big clue it had to do with Johnny.

It was the talk of the school.

I was in the stall in the bathroom when I heard a high-heeled clatter of entering girls.

"I think she's sleeping with that devil."

"You mean that homeless weirdo?"

"Who's a homeless weirdo?" (New voice.)

"Johnny Voodoo."

"Who's that?"

"You don't know him? That homeless psychedelic, you know, he lives in the park. Has that funky old accordion."

"I don't go to that park."

"Well, if you do go, don't mess with him, or he'll mess with you."

High-pitched squeals and laughter.

12

"Why would I mess with some funked-up old homeless guy?"

"Because he's fine."

"He's young."

"He's got voodoo you know where."

More squeals. A quick debate over whether or not Johnny was fly, cool, fine, dope, cranked, hot, mint, top, or so handsome he was sick.

"And besides," said a buttercream voice that had to belong to Claire Wright, "that Yankee slut has him."

When the smoke thinned and the high heels left, I went across the street to the fast-food place for a fish sandwich. Soon two girls I knew from algebra stood over my table.

"We just wanted to warn you," said Tanya. She's part black and has auburn curls around a pretty face. "You know, about Johnny Voodoo."

"He puts curses on people," said Aurora. She was a white girl with pale blue eyes, really straight, always wearing dresses below her knees. "They say he can vanish into thin air."

"Right," I said. "Sure."

"It's true," Tanya said. "We just thought you should know."

I unwrapped my sandwich and started taking

13

bites. Apparently everybody in Charmette was out of their brain.

The girls sat down.

Aurora popped the plastic lid off her cup of soda and started crunching on bits of ice while she talked.

"How long you been going with him?" Tanya said.

I laughed. "I'm not. I just met the guy this morning."

Aurora let out a big sigh of relief. "Then you've got to stay away from him," she said.

"He's like part Creole and part Native American," Tanya said. "Half his ancestors came over to settle Louisiana and the other half were here meeting the boat."

"So?" I said. "That's kind of nice."

"Yeah, it's nice," said Tanya, "if it don't make you crazy."

"Johnny's got a real crazy brother," Aurora said.

"He's got a dead brother!" Tanya said, shaking a finger in Aurora's face. "He killed himself seven years ago. You know he did!"

"They didn't find the body." Aurora twisted a pale strand of hair around her finger and chomped down on more ice.

"Probably because Johnny Voodoo did some sick ceremony with it. He was weird even back when he

14

was a little ten-year-old boy. He was in fifth when I was in fourth at Juliet Elementary. His mama and daddy died when he was real little, and he lived with his big brother."

"Yeah, I was at Juliet too." Aurora shook the last bit of ice into her mouth. "I was there the day they tried to put him in an orphanage."

"I saw that." Tanya nodded vigorously. "This car showed up for him and these two big ladies came walking back to the schoolyard with the principal. Everybody was talking about it. That Voodoo kid just ran over the fence. Too bad to be caught. He never came back to school, and we thought he was dead like his brother."

"You mean *you* thought his brother was dead," Aurora said. "I never did. There was no funeral."

"Whatever!" Tanya rolled her eyes. "You always want to turn everything into some kind of TV ghost story when it's scary for real. Anyway, *some* of us thought Johnny was dead, until one day he just showed up back in town, all grown and weird with that accordion thing. Nobody messes with him anymore."

"They're too scared," said Aurora. "And you should be too."

"Thanks for the warning," I said.

"We just wanted you to know."

"Really, thanks."

"We don't want them to find you dead someday."

They got up to go.

"I do appreciate that. Really."

"She's a goner," I heard Aurora tell Tanya as they walked away.

"Don't I know it," Tanya said. "Gone with the wind."

Chapter 2

All week long I've listened to them talking about Johnny Voodoo. And every bit of crap they put out only gets me more interested. It's been eight days since I've seen him.

It's the weirdest thing. We had no physical contact, except for that brief moment when his hand touched mine. We spent five minutes together.

But I can't stop thinking about him. The past few nights I've been having these intense dreams where we're looking into each other's eyes and communicating without talking.

I've had these out-there thoughts, like maybe he's an angel and my mom sent him down to look out for me. I've had this feeling I'm going to see him at any second. I had it walking to and from school. And I had it all weekend, even at the grocery store and doing the errands with my father. I kept expecting I'd see him at any second.

I have that feeling now, walking past the park. Every afternoon since I met him, the noisy green park pulls at me. The kids say he sleeps here, and I feel his presence so strongly I'm almost ready to go in. Almost but not quite.

There are always kids in the park after school. Little ones on the playground. Some high-school kids sitting under the magnolia trees and on the statues, making out and smoking cigarettes and laughing their low, slow, Southern laughs. Some of them drink beer. They get bums to buy it for them at the Home Comfort store.

I'd have killed for a park like this in my old neighborhood in the city. It's two blocks long and it's even got a tiny lake with swans.

If I see Johnny, I think I'd have the courage to go in.

If I go in there alone, I'll stand out like an alien. That's how I felt for a few weeks back in the city, like a newly landed wacko alien. It started the day after Mom died. No matter where I went, I felt exposed, as if everyone could tell that my life was forever changed. I felt like a shaved cat. That's my brother Kenny's latest expression. Something he picked up from junior high. Kenny's got friends because he already speaks in a sort of Charmette accent and we've been here less than two months. He has no problem going into the park.

18

It's called New Day Park, but it's open all night. The teenagers stay in the park partying all afternoon and late at night. Our street intersects with Olive, and I can hear the kids' whoops and screams and sometimes the driving, steady beat of a radio coming through my window at night. Sometimes I hear a cop car siren and then the noise stops for a while. I drift off only to be awakened by it sometime later. It's worse on Friday and Saturday nights, but there are kids out there every single night, making me wonder what I'm missing.

I also wonder what Johnny's doing. If he really sleeps in the park, I can't imagine how he can sleep with that racket going on. Maybe he parties with the kids.

Maybe he's already fallen in love with some other girl, somebody he spent more than six minutes with. I've been expecting to see him alone in the park, sitting on a branch of a tree or resting with his back against a statue, but maybe I should be looking for him with his arms around a girl and her arms around his neck, her hands in his hair.

I run my hand along the tall green stakes of the park fence, the way I used to run a Popsicle stick over the gates by Gramercy Park in the city when I was a little kid and my mom would buy me ice creams after school. Clackety-clack, don't look back.

I've counted each stake in the New Day Park

fence and there's forty-two before you get to the entrance in the middle of the block. Maybe that means I won't see Johnny for forty-two more days. Maybe—

It's him. Standing outside the gate, with his hat on his head and a smile in his eyes. Really him.

For the first time, I wonder if maybe the kids are right.

Maybe he is evil.

Maybe he is strange.

Well, he's definitely strange.

And I want to run, cross the street, and run away. Only I'm frozen.

He turns and starts to go in the park. Away from me.

My world gets dark.

He turns back.

He was picking a flower off a bush.

For me.

I take the flower as if I get them every day. "So, how are you?" Lame. I try again: "So, what's up, what's happening?"

"You," he says, nodding. "Can I walk you home?"

We walk. We don't talk. We cross Olive and turn onto Princessa. This guy is calm. He has this peacefulness that makes me feel like a skittery puppy running alongside its master. He grips my arm as we turn onto Princessa Street, which runs straight down into the woods that lead to the bayou. Not a hard grab, just a quick squeeze that sends a shot of electricity down my spine.

"You live down there?"

"Yeah, at the very end."

"Beautiful," he says, letting go of my arm. He looks at me sort of proudly, as if I not only live on Princessa Street but cleared off the land and built the house myself. I know he doesn't mean I'm beautiful, but it feels like it.

Johnny follows me right up onto the porch of our faded old house.

"I like your door," he says. The brilliant blue always makes me think of cartoons—the color so squeaky and fresh, standing out against the faded pink of the rest of the house.

"Curtis painted it," I say. "My dad."

"He's an artist," Johnny says.

"Yeah, he is." I wonder what else he can tell just from looking at the door. I wonder if he can tell Curtis is a creep. I can hear Curtis now, great roars of his laughter coming out from behind the house where he has his little painting studio. The last thing I want is for Johnny to meet my dad.

"So . . . ," I say. I don't want him to leave. I don't want him to stay. Curtis's laughter is getting louder. Go, Johnny. Don't go. Go.

Johnny lifts the brim of his hat and gives me a

21

quick wave. Some words almost come out of my mouth, what I used to say to my mother every time either one of us was going away for even a few hours, the words I never got to say to her in the very end: "Good-bye, I love you. . . ."

I've only seen him twice. Why do we have such an intense connection?

"Bye," I croak out. He's walking away; I have to say more.

"Hey, what's your last name?"

"Vouchamps," he says. "V-o-u-c-h-a-m-p-s." He pronounces it "Voo-sham." Then he says, with a little gleam in his eye, "It ain't Smith and it ain't Voo-doo."

"Cool," I say. "Very cool."

We wave again and then I force myself to go inside, where things are never very cool.

I go straight through the living room, which is dark and wrecked-looking. Old blankets and sheets nailed up over the windows instead of curtains. Makeshift coffee tables covered with newspapers and ashtrays overflowing with Curtis's butts. Clothes strewn around.

I throw a Sudden Urge tape onto the stereo to drown out the two noises.

One: the rhythmic *clunk, clunk, clonk!* above my head of Kenny lifting weights in his room. He gets home earlier than me, since he's in junior high. He hates the clutter of the living room even more than I do, and he goes straight up to his squeaky-neat room to lift his weights.

And two: Curtis laughing out back. He's been working on a new series of paintings—angels dressed like prostitutes. He's obsessed with his painting, goes out back all hours of the day and comes inside like a bear to its cave, only to drink, eat, and sleep. Sometimes he gets blocked and he can't paint and then you really have to watch out for him. You can tell he's blocked when the house fills up with more cigarette smoke than air and you see him pacing in the living room in the middle of the night, mumbling to himself.

He doesn't sound blocked now. He always uses real models to paint from and sometimes it's hard to tell whether he's more obsessed with his paintings or the models. Lately he's been using a tall, freckled idiot named Robyn. I know it's "Robyn" because she announced in her bossy little-girl voice: "It's Robyn with a *Y.*"

Whatever you say, bymbo.

Curtis always gets obsessed about things. That, or icy cold. The whole reason we came to live in Louisiana is he's obsessed with New Orleans. He talked about it before my mom got sick. Mom never wanted to leave our life in the city. She said his dreams were pipe dreams.

I always imagined these rusty old pipes with brown water coming out of them. And when we first arrived in New Orleans, in the heat of the summer, one month after Mom died, I felt as if I was living inside one of those pipes.

We lasted just two months in a two-room apartment; Curtis jammed two mattresses into a walk-in closet for Kenny and me. I can't tell you how humiliating it is to be sixteen years old and sleeping next to your brother. I hated the way Kenny smelled. Even though he bathed constantly and used every kind of mouthwash and deodorant, he had this underlying smell I couldn't stand. I hated hearing his breathing at night.

Sometimes I could hardly sleep. Once, when his snoring got real bad, I punched him. It had been years since he was little enough for me to beat up, but it was kind of satisfying getting in a little punch while he was sleeping. All he did was groan, roll over, and start up his snuffling elephant noises again. Curtis got to sleep on the couch in the living room. He tried to sell his work on the streets and went from gallery to gallery, but nobody cared that he'd been a big painter in New York. Nobody liked his abstract gray-and-black paintings. Everyone wanted things with a little more life and color. While we were on the road, the guy who handled Curtis's work in the city died. Curtis said it would be forever before they worked out the dealer's estate and went back to selling his paintings. Some old drunk told Curtis to forget about his old gray city paintings, move to Charmette, and study the colors of Louisiana.

So he did.

I thought about hitching back to New York and begging Marissa's mom to take me in, but I was too numb. I also thought about being abducted. I was dying to be one of those faces on a milk carton.

On the drive to Charmette, every time we stopped at a roadside diner or gas station, I'd imagine some nice lady taking one look at me and knowing I needed to be rescued. I played out that scene a thousand times in my head.

The lady (maybe with a nice husband and one or two small, well-behaved children) would spot me resting my head forlornly against the window of our beat-up car and she would open the door and gently take my hand. Then we would speed back to her penthouse apartment and she would show me my new, beautiful room, and the whole bad joke of my life would be over.

Only we didn't seem to run into a whole lot of elegant, compassionate women. I mostly saw big, loud families, creepy-looking guys in trucks, and powdery white and coal-black old people. And they looked at me as if I was weird. White trash.

If anything, they looked at Kenny as if he needed rescuing. Kenny must've been suffering in his own way, although you'd never know it on the outside. He always seems like some clean, perfect sitcom kid that was transferred into our family by mistake.

Kenny's way of dealing with life is to pretend it isn't happening. If he does feel anything, he keeps it all in.

Sometimes his coldness drove my mom nuts. He stopped running to her for comfort when he was seven years old. I was ten. Everything changed around our house the year I was ten.

Something big happened and I still don't know what it was. One day there was a huge fight between Mom and Curtis. Kenny was involved somehow. After that, everybody's personalities changed.

Mom got even closer to me. Kenny got weird. And Curtis stopped being Dad. I started calling him by his first name. It's as if we all had two lives, a kind of normal, warm life before and then the strange life that started that year.

I have a few memories from the Good Years: Mom and Dad kissing me good-night and leaving us with a baby-sitter. Me waking up sometime in the middle of the night because I hear soft music. I peek into the living room and see Mom in a lacy white dress, her hair all loose, and Dad in a dark jacket looking handsome, both of them twirling around and around to the music in the flickering light of three tall candles.

Or all of us on a picnic in Central Park by a lake. Kenny's just a baby, running around with a saggy diaper. Back then I still felt love and pride about him, mixed with the big-sister jealousy. We're all laughing a lot. Birds are chirping. We're throwing crusts to the squirrels. And Dad has a big yellow guitar and he's singing my favorite childhood song, "Puff, the Magic Dragon." He gets a tear in each eye when he gets to the sad part about the dragon not coming anymore because Little Jackie Paper's all grown up.

But most of my memories are from the Bad Years. Kenny hanging out with all his normal friends, acting like he wasn't part of our family when we all went out to dinner or to a museum, always walking a few steps behind or ahead of us. Curtis hardly ever talking to any of us, spending all his time in his downtown studio. Fights between Mom and Curtis over every model he ever used.

That's how she finally got into meditation. She got so wound up by my father and his models and Kenny and his coldness that she said she was going to get sick if she didn't do something to calm herself down. She did seem to be happier when she started meditating. But she got sick anyway. She got cancer.

Sometimes, when she was dying, it seemed as if my father might start to love her again. A few times he would go into her room with a book and I could hear the low rumble of his voice as he read to her. He brought her flowers sometimes and he carried her up to the roof once when she said she felt claustrophobic and needed air. But a lot of times he wouldn't even come home from the studio unless I called to say there was an emergency.

Curtis was good in emergencies, getting Mom to the hospital, calling the doctors, putting her in a cool, dark room when she was almost blind from the pain of a headache. He just wasn't good for all the things she needed every day.

After Mom got sick she didn't seem to care about the models anymore. She asked me only once—when she had just had a really high fever all night and was practically hallucinating—where he was. I called him at the studio that night and told him it was an emergency because she seemed to need him so much. By the time he got home she was sleeping and I thought he would be angry at me, but he just stood over her bed and looked at me with tears in his eyes. At that moment I could almost feel he was my real dad again.

Mom and I spent a lot of time together in her

room, before she was moved to the hospital. I cried a lot. Not around her, because it made her so sad, but when I was alone, especially at night. Kenny never cried, not even at her funeral.

One afternoon, two weeks after she took off, I exploded.

I'd only been back in school a week. I got all these weird looks from kids who didn't know what to say to me, and practically ended my friendship with Marissa because she burst into tears every time she saw me. Teachers tiptoed around me, even the mean ones. The one good thing about being back in school was I didn't have to be reminded of Mom every single second. Only every other second.

I used to walk the streets to avoid going home after school. Eventually I would have to let myself into our apartment, and then Mom was everywhere. In the pale lilac and cream walls of the apartment and in the little pencil marks she'd drawn inside the kitchen doorway each year on our birthdays to measure our growth; she was in the little plants and herbs in the kitchen windows, which she'd used in her stews and spaghetti sauces; she was in the soft patterned rugs on the floor, which she'd been so thrilled to find at an antique store during a country drive.

She was in the emptiness and quiet; she was in the air; she was behind the closed doors of the closets, where her clothes still hung, still carrying her scent.

But when I really needed to know that she had so recently been alive, I walked into her room and sat on her bed and looked at her dresser. On her dresser were all the things I had played with as a child—silk scarves, perfume bottles, dangling necklaces, a golden hairbrush, fancy cosmetics in shiny cases, our baby photos in tiny silver frames, a few flowers in a crystal vase. There were bits of clutter, like a sheet of my English homework and a ribbon from an old birthday present that was too pretty to throw away.

The dresser had also been crowded with her bottles of pills and medicines, but the good stuff had reassured me that someday she might just leap out of bed and start using all her old, wonderful things again.

I loved the big-framed mirror on the dresser. I used to sit on her bed and watch her brush her long hair and make funny faces.

On this particular afternoon, when I stepped into her room with that familiar feeling of dread and longing, all of it was gone. The only thing left of Mom was the mirror, and it looked strange and naked. Even our baby photos had been swept away, as if our baby selves had died with her.

I started shaking all over and then I cried. I was on the floor of their bedroom, still crying, when Curtis came home.

He reached out a hand and I growled. When I

could get my breath, I staggered to my feet and ran at him. "I want her things back!" I said, hitting at him until he grabbed my wrists. "Tell me what you did with them!"

He pulled a box from the closet and I ripped it open and put my face into it and held one of her scarves to my cheek. The scent of her was unbearable. I dragged the box to the dresser and I tried putting her things back exactly the way they had been. But it was no good. I felt as if he'd killed her.

Curtis stood watching me. I started quietly putting her things back in the box. I didn't know what I was doing. Curtis probably figured I'd calmed down, because he left the room.

"You bastard!" I screamed at him, loud enough to spread through the whole building. I threw a heavy picture frame and it missed his head and hit the wall. I kept screaming at him after I heard our apartment door slam behind him. I kept screaming even after Kenny stood in the doorway and stared at me. I screamed so long and so loud I couldn't talk the next day.

And after that I was too numb to deal with anything but the day-to-day stuff.

Until I met Johnny.

Chapter 3

I wish I had somebody to tell about Johnny.

I've still got his damp flower in my hand and I go to the kitchen sink to fill up a jar. Through the kitchen window I see Robyn posing half naked in our backyard. White, white skin with tiny liver-colored freckles everywhere. Teased-up hair that's bleached white.

And there's Curtis, pacing in front of his easel.

He stops.

"You gotta have the face of an angel." He throws Robyn a rag. "Wipe off that whorish mouth!"

She pouts as she wipes off her red lipstick, then throws the rag in Curtis's face. He shakes with hoarse laughter. I crank up Sudden Urge even more.

I go upstairs and do my homework, stopping every six seconds to think about Johnny. The way his hair looked in the light; the way his hand felt when he grabbed my arm. His beautiful voice. The shine in his eyes. His exotic last name. It takes me about fifty hours to do my work.

This is dinner at our house: I'm putting frozen macaroni-and-cheese dinners into the oven. Kenny, drawn by hunger and perhaps a tiny need for a bit of company, is sitting at the table reading an economics book. Curtis and Robyn come bursting through the kitchen door.

Curtis is wearing a jean jacket over his painting clothes, smelling so strongly of turpentine and cigarettes he makes my eyes sting. He has an arm slung around Robyn's shoulder. He's got that merry attitude as if he's a bad boy and I'm his mother or something.

"We're going to do the oyster number," he says. That means they're going to stay out all night eating raw oysters, drinking in bars, and probably going to her place.

Kenny looks up from his book and blinks.

"Fine," I say. I get real busy with the dial of the stove.

Robyn laughs through her nose. "Well, don't miss us too much, y'all."

"I've got such weird kids," Curtis tells Robyn as they leave.

I don't even feel it when he says things like that. He's just a guy who pays the rent.

Now all I have to deal with is Kenny.

There's something so vulnerable about him, sitting there reading, waiting for me to tell him to set the table. Good-looking TV kid with a baseball cap; large, square hands holding his book. He would never admit that he needs me—he probably doesn't even know it himself. But if I just did something unexpected, like walking out of the house or throwing his macaroni and cheese at him, I have this feeling he'd totally fall apart. I can't believe I'm having such cruel thoughts, but Kenny brings them out in me. I know he doesn't ask me for anything, but sometimes I'm so crushed by guilt over not doing more for him that the guilt gets all twisted up and it comes out like hatred. Love and hate, that's what I feel. And what it all adds up to is putting down our trays of dinner and sitting there forcing myself to be nice.

"How is school?" I ask.

"Fine."

"How's the soccer team?"

"We're starting practice next week and—" Here he gets excited for a second, and I hate that little-kid excitement because he's not a little kid. I mean, he's got fifteen pounds and a few inches on me. I focus in on a red zit on his otherwise perfect skin and I sort of glare at him until he interrupts himself and says, "It's fine. It's fine, Deirdre."

I give him tons of whipped cream on his chocolate pudding even though he doesn't ask. And he volunteers to do the dishes even though it's my turn. It's all we can do for each other.

That night in bed, I listen to the night birds and croakers in the woods and the noise of far-off radios and cars cruising up the street. No sounds of an accordion anywhere. I imagine how it will be when Johnny and I first kiss. If we ever kiss. Maybe we'll have sex.

I had sex once, and the memory of it jolts me.

His name was Brett O'Brien, but everyone called him Brew, because he was into drinking beer. He was the last guy I ever thought I'd end up with. He was two years older, my friend Dana's big brother. He was kind of a jock type, not into music or any of the things my crowd was into.

It just happened one night when I slept over at Dana's. Marissa was there too. It was before Mom went into the hospital and she said it'd been a long time since I'd been to a sleepover and I deserved to have fun.

The night started out great: watching R-rated videos, raiding Dana's parents' fridge. (They were out of town and they trusted us because we were good girls.) I had on kind of a sexy nightgown in this slippery black fabric. And we were all trying on makeup and perfume. I guess I looked pretty good, because Brett kept walking by our room and sneaking looks. Late that night, after we'd talked about every male-related topic we could think of, Marissa and Dana fell asleep and I couldn't. I went down to the kitchen and Brett was there, sitting at the kitchen table with a beer.

He opened up a bag of chips and gave me a beer, but it tasted too awful to drink so I just sat and talked with him. He was an okay guy. He seemed to be, anyway. We talked about all kinds of stuff and he looked sort of cute. I mean, just the fact that there was this older guy interested in me made him look even cuter. And then suddenly he asked if he could kiss me.

It was a good kiss. I'd had a few real kisses before and this one was probably the best. Not too wet or scary. He started running his hands along my neck and I felt like I wanted him to touch me even more.

That's why I said yes when he asked if we could just go upstairs and lie on his bed together for a while. He said just to talk. He looked at me as if he really loved me. In fact, that's what he said: "You know, Deirdre, I think I could fall in love with you."

It seems totally brain-dead now, but I believed him.

We went upstairs and we talked some more and

we kissed some more, being real quiet so we didn't wake the others. And all of that was fine. It was great. And then we were having sex.

The whole thing was nothing like I'd imagined. All I felt was a little bit of pain—such a dull, strange feeling, like someone hitting their hand against your hand over and over again. There was no excitement to it, no sensation. But he felt plenty. He was grunting and panting and I was so afraid he'd wake the others. It was all over really quick and the sheets were pretty messed up. He was kind of nervous and polite afterward, asking if I was okay. We didn't kiss. In fact we barely even talked again. I slipped back into Dana's room. When I saw Brett eating Cheerios in the morning and he gave me a wink, I felt nothing for him.

The worst part of the whole pitiful experience was worrying about AIDS. I got so worried, I finally told Marissa and she was totally shocked. She went with me to this health clinic we found in the yellow pages and they took blood from my arm and that was really scary. Then they gave me a number (I still remember it—5687) and told me to come back in a week for my results. The whole testing process was supposed to be anonymous, but the number made me feel like somebody's turn at the butcher's. When they told me the results and I told Marissa, she dug her nails into my arm so hard I had the marks for a week.

Negative. That's good, I had to tell her. Negative is *good.*

After I got the results, and after I got my period, I told Mom about the whole thing. I had to. She'd always made me promise to tell her when I'd had my first time. We talked for hours. She wasn't mad. But she said she was disappointed in me that I hadn't used AIDS precautions or even thought about birth control. I told her I had thought plenty about it but hadn't exactly planned that moment with Brett. She made me promise that in the future I would be careful. She said she knew that my next time would be different, that next time I would sleep only with someone I really loved. Someone who had proved to be a real friend. Just her saying that made it true somehow.

I fall asleep wondering if Johnny's going to be a real friend. Somewhere, far away, beyond the night sounds and park noise, I hear Mom. And she's telling me something about Johnny, something reassuring and good, but I can't quite make it out because I'm drifting, drifting. . . .

Chapter 4

Time to hit the showers after gym at Charmette High: Big naked girls prance about, stepping into the steamy stalls, whacking each other's butts with wet towels, hooting about various boys. They slip into bright panties and bras slowly and casually, as if they were alone in their own bathrooms.

Of course, not all of us are leaping about, gaily shedding our clothes. I am not always shy, but when I am, I tend to suffer from what Marissa called *pathological shyness*. Sometimes it happened at sleepovers in the city when I just wouldn't feel like stripping in front of someone's older sister. Sometimes it happened when I had to walk past a guy I liked, and my limbs would suddenly refuse to move in a normal way. And sometimes it happened when a teacher called on me in class and for no reason at all I would feel my face get hot and red, and I'd have to pretend I was having a coughing fit.

I didn't have these attacks too often. The problem is, I did on my first day at Charmette High. And it kind of stuck.

A few SWAGs came up to me at lunch my first day and asked me to talk. Their accents were so thick I could hardly understand them.

"Just say something, Yankee girl." Liz Haddonfield was in my face.

"What do you want me to say?"

And then they cracked up and imitated me in these really stiff, exaggerated accents, like they were talking with marbles in their mouths. If I had been in the right mood I could have laughed along or at least given a little okay-you-had-your-fun-now-beat-it smirk, but the whole cafeteria seemed weird. I felt kind of claustrophobic and unreal and I had a lump in my throat the size of a fist.

A couple of the girls said I sounded just like someone from some TV show, and they asked me to say something else. All I could do was shake my head. I mean, there was this little crowd around me, and they probably didn't plan to be cruel, but I felt as if I were some little robot onstage. I could not do it.

Liz Haddonfield said to everyone: "The little Yankee brat just thinks she's too good for us. And in that little Yankee outfit of hers. Don't you, Yankee?"

I was wearing a sleeveless black cotton dress that

came to my ankles. Two things they didn't do here: black, and below-the-knee.

I couldn't talk because I didn't want to cry. I just let them think I was stuck up.

And now, seven weeks later, I'm still not talking. And I do not want to get undressed for the shower.

Liz Haddonfield's standing in her jeans and purple bra, one leg up on a bench, talking in her husky drawl to Claire Wright: "You won't believe what happened to Matt last night. His dad busted him when he took the car to come by and see me—"

"I know all about it," Claire says. She's not quite as tall as Liz, but they're both black-haired belles, giantesses compared to me, with bodies straight out of *Playboy.*

"Steve was telling me this morning . . ."

Ms. Brightley, our phys ed teacher, is prowling around making sure everyone showers. Otherwise I'd just throw my baggy jeans and sweatshirt on over my sweaty blue gym outfit.

In a far, dark corner, Tanya and Aurora are taking turns holding up a towel and getting undressed behind it. At the beginning of the year, the SWAGs used to make fun of them, but now they're onto other business.

Usually I have an elaborate routine of holding up my towel with one hand, undressing with the other hand, running to the shower, checking to see if any-one's looking, slipping off the towel at the last second, ducking under the spray long enough for Brightley not to get pissed, then grabbing the towel, going to my locker, and slipping my stuff back on while I hold it around me. I try to be the last person in the shower so that most of the kids will be gone by the time I get out. When I get through the whole routine safely, I can't even describe the relief.

No such luck today. I'm halfway there, naked un-der the towel, about to step into the shower. I shoot a look back at the black-haired belles, expecting to see them all dressed and yakking their way out the door. But they're still half naked, sitting on the bench by the lockers now, silent and watching me with big cold eyes.

Ms. Brightley catches me standing there. "Is there a problem here? Better get a move on, young lady."

What else can I do? I slip off the towel, jump in that shower, and then watch my towel get yanked off the top of the stall.

Even above the hiss of the steamy shower spray, I can hear them: "Let's see her walk her scraggly little Yankee Voodoo butt out here now!"

"Maybe Johnny can build her up. Do some voo-doo on her boobs!"

"Man, she needs help everywhere."

"He should start on her face—she is ugleee."

"With that big old nose."

"And that nasty space between her teeth, like an old jack-o'-lantern."

"Hoo, yeah."

Then I hear barking. Howling.

I take the longest shower of my life. I'm in there with tears stinging my eyes, hugging my body, believing everything they're saying even though I'm telling myself they're just jerks, that they should just get a life. I feel ugly from the inside out.

My chest seems flat as a board. My nose seems as big as Pinocchio's. And my teeth. I've always loved my teeth. Mom used to say the little gap between my teeth was appealing. I never knew it made me look like a pumpkin.

The water's so hot it's turning my skin red. I wish it would just burn me. Kill me. Or make me black out and send me into a coma.

"Enough of that," Ms. Brightley is yelling. Where has she been? She probably heard everything. "Everybody get moving."

She raps on the door of my stall. "You in there, what's going on? This is not a spa. Finish up and get on out!"

I turn off the water. I will not cover my body with my hands. I will walk out and pretend I didn't hear a word. I'll pretend I didn't notice that my towel was yanked away. I will pretend I'm normal. I won't open my mouth. I won't walk bent over, trying to hide my pitiful chest. I . . .

There's no one out there but Ms. Brightley, tapping her foot. She hands me a towel.

"It's just normal girl talk," she tells me in her drill sergeant voice. "You'll get used to it."

"Gold Dust, Paradise, Kickapoo, Tallulah . . ." Walking home, by the park, I hear his voice behind me. Half chanting, half singing. It sounds like a rope-skipping rhyme. I slow down and the back of my neck prickles with excitement, even though I'm feeling so ugly I don't really want to see him. I know I have the same face I had when I last saw him, but now it feels unspeakably hideous. His voice is warm in my ear: "Sugartown, Tickfaw, Violet, Zylks! What're you doing, Deirdre?"

"Nothing," I say. And then: "Hi."

"Hi, yourself," he says.

I can't even look at him. Well, just sneak a look, but I feel too ugly to have him look at me. I just keep walking. He keeps walking too, his accordion clunking between us.

"What were you singing?" I say, watching my feet moving on the sidewalk.

"Towns," he says. "Magical names of Louisiana

44

towns. None of them more magic than Charmette, because that's the one where you live." He slows his pace. "Hey, what's wrong?"

"Nothing."

He scoots around in front of me and blocks my path. "Deirdre," he says. "Look at me."

I look at him. And he doesn't go into shock. He doesn't pull back in disgust and horror. He's smiling and nodding. "Okay," he says. "Thank you. I feel better now."

I feel a little better too. We turn onto my street.

"Listen," he says. "I want to take you somewhere. I want to show you something. Right near your house." He points to the woods. "I mean . . . only if you can go." He seems suddenly shy.

"Definitely," I say. We are at my house. "Like when?"

"Now," he says.

I want to run off with him. Anywhere, anytime, forever. Only not right this particular second. Right this second I need to stand in front of the bathroom mirror and fix my face up. I feel as if I've been damaged and I need to make some repairs.

"Can we do this in, like, an hour?" I say.

Silence. And then: "Sure," he says. "Absolutely."

We plan to meet outside my place.

*   *   *

45

It's not a bad face. It's sort of friendly and sad. The eyes are a brownish green with gold flecks and long, dark lashes. The nose is not too big. It's not a pert little cheerleader nose turned up at the end, but it goes pretty good with the face. The mouth is okay. Not too big, not too little, with a curve people call a Cupid's bow. But open that mouth and—man—Pumpkin City.

Okay, close the mouth and check out the rest. Hair, okay. Light brown with blond streaks. Falls straight to the shoulders. Bangs could use cutting. A plain style. Try lifting the hair up in a bun. Gross. Forget the hair.

Have to climb up on the edge of the bathtub to see the rest in the mirror. There they are. Or aren't. Put on a clean button-down denim shirt and a black leather vest over that. Rest of the body, okay. Black jeans. Skinny legs. Turn around (not easy to do on the slippery, narrow end of the tub) and look over shoulder at the rear view. Not bad either. The kind of rear view a ballerina might have.

Rapid knocking.

"Hon. I gotta get in, gotta pretty myself, Daddy's orders!"

"Just a sec."

"Sugar, I don't have a second, I gotta tinkle!" Robyn rattles the door.

"Okay, okay," I say through gritted teeth. I open

46

the door and start to slink out. She blocks my way with a giant flowered bag.

"You can finish up," she tells me. "I'm not shy."

I figure I might as well grab the lip gloss. I ignore her sitting on the toilet and dig around some more and find it. I unscrew the little jar and—

"Whoa!" She leaps off the toilet. "What do you think you're doing?"

"Putting on lip gloss. Is that okay with you?"

"That is the wrong shade, doll," she says with a flush of the toilet. "If you want to catch a man, you're gonna need some real work on that face."

In spite of myself, I get interested. Still, I say, "I don't want to catch a man."

"Oh, you got one already?" We're looking at each other in the mirror. My face tells all.

"Oh, you got one, all right," she says. "And from the looks of things, you got it bad. You're off to see him right now, aren'tcha?"

I shake my head. "No way."

"Mm-hmm," she says. She unzips her enormous bag and props it next to the sink. It's stuffed with every sort of cosmetic brush and tube and can and container you can imagine.

"Let's start with that mouth," she says. And before I can protest, she's taking out a sharp red pencil and holding my head still with one hand and drawing just outside the line of my lips. My mouth is parted and she sees my teeth and says, "Don't worry yourself about those teeth. When you get yourself a rich honey he'll pay a good dentist to get them capped. In the meantime, we'll want to draw attention away from this mouth." She fills it in with a shocking magenta.

"We're gonna want to downplay that nose, too," she says, swiftly drawing two beige-pink smears along the sides of my nose.

"And we'll have to highlight your eyes, emphasize them. Close 'em."

She's coming at me with tools in both her hands, her fingers flying, her long silver nails flashing. I think it best just to comply. When I open my eyes again, I see bright blue on the lids ("It sets off the green, sugar"), a thick black line on the top, and stiff black mascara.

To finish me off, she whooshes some powdered rouge on my cheeks and then vigorously rubs it into my skin with the heel of her hand. "The illusion of bone structure," she says.

But the only illusion I see is that the circus seems to be in town. My face is a clown mask.

"Now you look all pretty for your date," she tells the clown. "You should be thanking me. A job like this would cost you big at a beauty salon."

"Thank you," says the clown.

"Don't tell me you don't have a date."

"I don't."

"You know, you got yourself a fellow, you gotta have him take you somewhere nice. High-class."

Like the oyster-and-beer bars she goes to with Curtis?

"What kind of car does he have, sugar?"

"I don't know," says the clown. "I mean, there isn't a guy!"

She drops the girlie-girl voice and says, "Honey, I don't know what you're trying to pull, but it ain't gonna be my leg. I been around, and if there's no guy, then I'm your granny."

I grab a tissue and run downstairs, swiping at my face as I go, catching one last look at myself in the dusty hall mirror, swiping a little bit more. I can almost live with the results. Now I just look like a clown who got caught in a rainstorm. But maybe that's an improvement. And if it isn't, it's too late to wash it all off, because Johnny'll be outside at any second and the last thing I want is for Robyn to see him.

We push through the woods fast. Johnny leads the way on an invisible path. I'm out of breath. My shoes sink into the mud, and I shiver in the damp gloom. Not too romantic.

49

"Watch out for the knees," Johnny says. He grabs my hand and pulls me along.

"What are you talking about?" I ask, almost tripping for the millionth time on one of the knobby things sticking up from the ground.

"Cypress knees," he says, pausing for just a second, sweeping his arm up at the big cypress trees. "The knees are aboveground roots. The trees like to breathe." And then we're moving on.

Usually I don't care about the names of trees and things, but the warm feeling I have holding his hand extends to his words. They'll stay in my brain forever, like the memory of his touch.

Finally we come to a little clearing just before the water. The gloom of the woods is broken up by long shafts of sun, and here the tall cypresses and oaks are hung with long, trailing bits of gray-green Spanish moss. There's an ancient, still feeling in the woods. Johnny pulls me down beside him on a fallen log.

He gives my hand a quick squeeze, rubs his thumb over the top, and then lets go.

"You come into the woods much?" he says.

"Not really." Curtis took Kenny and me back here to show us the bayou the day we first moved in. I remember Curtis's arm heavy across my shoulders, and the still, creepy waters. I just wanted to get away.

"You see this stuff?" Johnny says, jumping up and

grabbing off the lacy end of some dangling Spanish moss. "There's a Native American myth about it. . . ."

He sits back beside me, touching the moss. I feel the soft ends, my hand near his hand. I want to touch the long tendon running along the inside of his wrist. I want to feel his arms around me. I want him to kiss me. I just keep feeling the moss between my fingers.

"A girl with a beautiful, open soul was about to get married to the first person she'd ever really loved," he tells me. "An enemy tribe killed her during the wedding. The guy she was going to marry was insane from losing her. He cut off her hair and hung it from an oak tree that grew by her grave. The strands of her hair blew from tree to tree and still hang from the branches like a gift for anyone who never lived to have love in their lives."

"Wow," I say. It's a beautiful, sad story, but what really gets to me is all the times he used the word *love,* looking at me as he talked, not seeming embarrassed at all, like most boys would be. It's almost as if he's telling me that we won't end up like that sad couple, that we'll live to see a real love happen between us.

Or maybe he's just telling a story. Sometimes I believe things are real because I so badly want them to be.

"You know," he says to me now, "I—please don't take this wrong, but you . . ."

God, he's going to say, "You and I should just be friends," or "You shouldn't get hung up on me, babe." Or . . .

"What?" I ask. "Just tell me!"

"Okay," he says. "You're so beautiful."

I get all red and look away.

"Wait . . . ," he says. "That's not all."

Now what? You're so beautiful but I don't want to be your boyfriend? You're so beautiful but you could use some dental work?

"What I mean is, why are you wearing that stuff on your face?"

Actually, what did I expect? It would be bizarre if he *didn't* notice.

I have no idea what to say.

"Deirdre." He leans in close to me, touching my face, with a melting look of concern, as if he's helping some baby animal in a trap. "I didn't mean to insult you. Maybe you like that stuff on your face. I don't know what's wrong with me."

He pulls back and sort of rocks in an agitated way.

"No, it's me, Johnny," I say. "I'm the one who's got something wrong with me." Then I blurt: "I just felt so ugly today and my father's bimbo girlfriend slapped all this goop on my face and . . . Anyway, thanks. I mean for saying I'm—you know."

"You are," he says, wiping some of the stuff off my face with a wet leaf. "Beautiful. With or without paint. There's not one ugly thing about you."

He puts down his accordion and stands in front of me. Then he grabs my hands and pulls me to my feet. My heart's slamming in my chest. He moves back a few feet, his eyes locked with mine, raises his arms to the sky, throws back his head, and inhales deeply. He grins at me.

"Come on," he says. "I want to teach you something. About real beauty. Breathe."

Breathing exercises are not exactly what I had in mind. I hate that kind of New Age hippie crap.

"Breathe," he commands.

I take a tentative, quiet sniff, taking in the damp moss, the sweet honeysuckle and jasmine, the wet-dog smell of nearby water, but I can't snort in a big breath. No way.

"Do it!" he says. Part of me feels pissed off, but the other part is curious. I want to know what it is he wants me to know.

And then I'm just doing it. I'm breathing, he's breathing. His eyes close. I close mine.

"Do you feel it?" he says real low.

"I don't know."

"Breathe," he says. "Do you?"

"I think—"

"Do you?"

"Yes, okay, I . . ." I'm like a tree or something, rooted into that spot, a strong current of something filling up all the atoms and molecules of my body.

"You feel it?" he says again.

"Yes, damn it, yes!"

"Well, that's good, damn it, that's good," he says.

My eyes burst open and his are open. The air seems newly charged with light and color and stillness. I'm laughing, he's laughing.

"And now feel the power of above," he says. "Close your eyes, Deirdre, breathe in the energy from the stars, the sun, the heavens. Let your body flood with light. And when you breathe out, let your whole self go out with your breath. Let yourself just go."

I'm breathing. I'm feeling. I'm imagining light filling me up, the way Mom used to do when she meditated. I never could do it with her, but now: light, warmth, a kind of wild freedom—that's what I feel out there in the woods with Johnny.

"Your whole life is in that breath in and that breath out, Deirdre. And tell me how . . ." I feel his hands on my shoulders and open my eyes to see his dark, serious stare.

His voice is soft.

"How could that be anything but beautiful?"

I say nothing. There is so much in his eyes. "You are so beautiful, Deirdre," he says.

And I believe him. The way I believe people I've really trusted in my life, like Mom. It's as if he's taken in every single part of me and he's seeing me exactly the way I am. I'm standing there all exposed, and for once in my life the truth is out. For the first time in a very long time I feel comfortable inside and out. Standing and breathing in the woods with the clown makeup half wiped off my face, I feel as if Johnny has shown me myself.

Chapter 5

We didn't kiss that day. He walked me straight home.

But the feeling of what happened in the woods is still with me the next day. It's still there in school, giving me a shot of courage when I have to use the bathroom after lunch.

Right around noon is when you want to avoid the bathroom, unless you're a SWAG or a Triple A. The Triple As come in either sex and they're African Americans with Attitude. I first heard it when this group of black girls put together a band called the Triple As.

I use the name for all the black kids you wouldn't want to mess with. The ones who wear the latest jazz style with the geometric patterns and the stacked-heel shoes. The Triple As mostly don't hang with white kids, except for a few who talk black and pretend they have black blood.

It's totally pitiful. This girl Anita's whiter than me, with hair so straight it looks ironed, but she talks as if she's black and she insists her father was black. It's possible, but I kind of doubt it. In a way I can relate to Anita. If I were forced to choose between hanging with the SWAs and the Triple As, I guess I'd pretend to be black too. Not all the black kids are Triple As and not all the white kids are SWAs. There's a bunch of kids—white and black and Creole and from mixed backgrounds—who are potheads, pseudohippies, punks, glitterati, rockabillys, swampheads, and marsh dogs. And then there's the geeks who hang in the computer club or in some other weird group. Zebras are what the SWAs and Triple As sometimes call the white and black kids who hang out with each other. Like Tanya and Aurora. Or maybe they just call the half white–half black kids zebras. I haven't figured out the fine points yet.

The Triple As smoke and drink like the SWAs, but they don't go screaming through the hall smashing lockers. They've got a deadly air to them. They're my age but I feel as if they're older, as if they've seen so much they're already thirty.

The Triple As don't give me any trouble. If anything, I feel connected to them because they hate the SWAs. Years ago there was some kind of fight between the SWAs and the Triple As and somebody ended up getting killed. Since then they barely deal with each other, although sometimes there's a quick shove in the hallway, or something happens in the bathroom.

The Triple A girls are braver than the SWAGs. If a Triple A girl doesn't like the way a SWAG looks at her, the Triple A girl will turn to her friend and say something like "Who's that cracker looking at?" And the SWAG and her friends don't do anything, until the Triple As leave and then the SWAG will get all brave and say something like "that slut thinks she's so bad."

Right around lunch is when they get to the bathroom, take hits off joints and cigarettes, and put on makeup. The Triple As hang out by the windows and the SWAGs by the door, each group staking out half of the long, cracked mirror above the sinks.

So you don't want to be in the bathroom at that time, unless you're somebody like Jane. Jane is the last person you'd expect to have that name.

I didn't even know she was a she until I first saw her in the bathroom one morning, brushing her teeth. She's taller than any girl at school, at least six-two. She has short hair; hooded eyes; black, black skin, and no makeup. She dresses in the same neat clothes every day, black jeans and a white button-down shirt. She is so bad she can do anything she likes, like brushing her teeth in the middle of a SWAG convention. She's quiet in the history class I have with her. She gets good grades. She brings huge, delicious meals—gumbos, fried shrimp, salads, jars of lemonade—and eats them on the school steps with real silverware. She's got high, jutting cheekbones and long, skinny legs.

I've seen her some mornings just as I'm arriving, getting let out of a pearl-gray expensive-looking car and waving good-bye to a light-skinned fat man I once heard her call Daddy. She hangs with no one and she's probably the only person I like in this school. There have been times when I had a sudden feeling we'd be friends. But she mostly scares me, even though she never looks my way. She's got this cool, quiet dignity that reminds you of somebody on death row. She looks as if she might be armed. I'd bet a million dollars that you could set a bomb off two feet away from her and she wouldn't jump.

Jane's the first person I see when I have to pee so bad that I take the risk of stepping into the bathroom at high noon. Jane's washing her hands, looking at her face in the mirror, standing smack in between the SWAGs and the Triple As, the only quiet thing in that room because everyone's roaring.

Usually I'd get hit with a wave of terror, but now I have that new calm inside me.

I left the woods with that calm yesterday and woke up with it this morning. It's something like being in love, but I don't feel all jittery. I used to have this feeling when I was little and I'd have long talks with Mom at our kitchen table after Kenny went to bed, while Curtis was downtown painting late in his studio. It'd be just me and Mom and she made me feel as if she understood whatever was going on with me and she was there for me.

The calm is like a thin sheet of gauze between me and the world, protecting me, filtering out some of the fear.

It's almost as if Jane can sense my new state because her eyes catch mine in the mirror. I don't see warmth but I don't see hostility either. I see a sort of recognition.

I go into the stall and pee. When I'm done I head out and that's when Husky Haddonfield says, "Aren't you going to wash your hands, Yankee Voodoo?"

The other SWAGs are laughing, nudging each other. The Triple As are quiet, watching. Even Jane, who was just about to leave, looms big before the door waiting to see what I'm going to do.

"You know what?" I say to Haddonfield. I'm trying to think of the most New York curse, the most New York *thing* I can pull here. I mean, what would the lead singer of Sudden Urge do? And then it comes to me. "You know what? Why don't you just jump on this?"

I show her my middle finger. I don't do it like

some little trembly jerk, either. I do it slow and relaxed with a casual smile.

The SWAGs are laughing. The Triple As are nodding with approval, smiling and saying to each other: "Yeah, that baby won't *take* no stuff." Jane gives me a wink and a nod and then slips out the door.

Liz Haddonfield and her little twin, Claire Wright, are the only ones not laughing. Wright gets up in my face and says, "You better watch yourself, bitch."

And still no fear. That gauze around me, and I know all this crap is temporary. I know it the way I know anything, that it's not going to matter tomorrow and it doesn't matter now. I smell the stink of her perfume. I look at her, say nothing, think about how pale her eyes are and how clumpy and tacky her mascara looks. How she has a slightly double chin when she bends her head down, glaring at me, and how she's going to be ugly when she's older. How they'd use her big, rubbery pink body as a trampoline in the mosh pit of a New York club. Finally she backs off. And then and only then do I walk away. Slowly.

After school I just think of Johnny and there he is. Sky's green and gloomy and he's way back against the park gate, hat over his eyes, big strange silver accordion hanging off his shoulder. He sees me and he's running, holding his hat on his head, the accordion flying.

Then he catches himself and slows to a walk. Moving with all the time in the world, his eyes the color of night, breathing me in. There's no gauze in place now. It's shredded, gone, invisible. How come he makes me feel so much I feel sick?

Today we go straight to the woods after I throw my books on the porch.

"I'm going to take you for a ride," he says.

He drags a small rowboat out from some bushes by the bayou's swampy edge. I don't want to get in, until he puts his accordion down in the middle.

The surface of the bayou looks like an emerald carpet. Seems solid as a pool table. You'd walk right on top of it and drown if you didn't know better, because it's covered with eighty thousand little bits of duckweed. We slide over that carpet to where the water starts showing through, a blackish green. Late-afternoon sun slants through the trees. Mist sits on the water like a ghostly silver cloud. The light catches in all the hanging Spanish moss and makes the place feel like an ancient dinosaur breeding ground. A few skinny brown pelicans fly by, looking like pterodactyls.

Johnny's rowing, watching my face, as if he's endlessly fascinated by every new thing I'm taking in.

Being so close to him, on the rocky boat with just the accordion between us, out on this scary bit of swamp, I'm having one of those I-can't-look-at-him moments. And he knows it.

"Look at me, girl."

I look; then my eyes dart away. He laughs. Puts down an oar, reaches out his warm hand, touches my cold hand. Puts down the other oar. Takes both my hands.

"Why can't you look at me?"

"I can," I say. Then I can't.

He pulls his hands away. But he's not mad, just picking up the oars, steering us around a narrow bend, following the slow current. I dip my hand in the water. It feels as thick and warm as recently cooled soup.

Squawks and end-of-the-earth sounds split the air. I look at him now.

He tilts his head to the side, nodding, nodding.

"Love," he says. "Do you know about love?"

I'm New York. I'm cool. I'm the jump-on-this girl. I know how to breathe in the moon and the ground. We're in this corny romantic setting in a boat and he's asking me about love, but I can deal.

"I know about pain," I say.

"Pain goes away," he says.

"So does love," I say.

"You're wrong," he says. "Love is the only thing

that never dies. It has to find its own way, but it never goes. Real love doesn't."

"How do you know?"

"Because I—" He stops and his eyes are dazed, his lips slightly parted, as if he's seen some wonder. He's going to say *because I love you.* Only he says: "Because I do."

"Oh," I say. And then we head back.

Chapter 6

Mornings used to be killers. Sometimes there would be one blank second of grace before the knowing. In the beginning, I would wake after three or four hours of sleep and it would still be dark in the apartment and I would know.

Your mother is dead. Your mother is gone. It happened. She's gone. You're here. And you have to get up.

Get up. Do everything you used to do. Stand in the shower. The water falling senseless on your body. Towels, clothes, putting toast in the toaster. All of it flat, pointless.

All of it the same only different, because Kenny's cooking his own eggs, checking to be sure he has his homework ready, sitting with the back of his neck exposed, reading the back of the juice carton the way he always does. But now there's a streak of dirt on his neck and you hate him for that streak, you want to shove his face into his eggs until he can't breathe, for that streak.

There was no Mom, grouchy as she used to be in the morning, laughing at her own tiredness.

I got used to the mornings, the way you'd get used to anything. Moving to New Orleans helped. Everything was so loud and new and jumbled, there was no place to notice her absence. There was no memory of her in the physical parts of the mornings, not in the kitchen or the bathroom.

Just in my heart and my arms and my stomach. I'd remember one tiny, glistening thing—"Dee, I saved up and I am going to get you those red boots"—or a storm of things: her soft voice, her rock-out dancing in the kitchen, her blue Italian plates; her laughing with a friend on the phone, her turning the pages of a magazine, her drinking a cup of coffee, telling me I'm a gourmet, a wonder girl, an angel for making it for her. All those Sunday afternoons we spent in museums and then ducked out from their slow, musty warmth into the rainy streets, splashing down the stairs, running, Mom making me use my ear-splitting whistle to get us a cab. Bam. Gone.

And nobody can ever tell you how it's going to be. I saw her dying. I knew she was leaving. And still I didn't have a clue.

On this morning, the empty quiet in the house

feels good. There's birdsong and sounds of slamming car doors, barking dogs. My bedroom upstairs is filled with a white, clean light. Through the laces curtain (which I stole into my suitcase from our old apartment) the sun comes all sparkling and warm against my white walls and the dark wood floor.

Not twenty-four hours after we moved in, Curtis brought in a sander and blasted the old paint off the floors and then sandpapered them by hand, working so hard I thought he was going to have a heart attack. The dark honey-colored wood came out and he polished it until it glowed and then poured too much slick shiny stuff on it. Some of the wood in the house still sucks at your feet.

The only colors in my room are the pink and silver of the sleeping bag on my bed and a little blue dab of paint on the wall next to my bed. I had taken what was left of the cartoon-blue door paint and intended to paint my whole room that color. But after one quick slap with my brush I decided it would be too sad.

It was her favorite color, but it makes a room so dark. The paint splat's shaped like a comet or a sheep or sometimes a woman with a veil on her head. Now it looks like a comet.

Kenny's already gone on to school and I feel a strange squeeze of something in my heart when I see his dish rinsed out in the sink. I'm suddenly starving and wolf down a quick scrambled egg on a toasted English muffin. It tastes better than anything I ever remember eating.

And standing right outside my door, like a rainbow, is Johnny.

We can't get these fool grins off our faces. We throw our arms around each other on this green morning birdsong street and hug.

Then we walk, hand in hand, and have our first normal conversation.

"What's your life like in that house?" he says.

"It's okay." I say. And then: "My mother died six months ago."

His hand automatically tightens around mine, so hard it's all I can feel.

"Oh, baby," he says. "She must've loved you so much."

And those words crush me inside. My legs almost give out from the pain of those words. Because it's true. She did. As much as I loved her, it's the way she loved me, like no one else in the world, as if she were going to be here forever.

I know he feels everything, somehow knows what I've lost. I can't talk about her now. He knows and I don't have to explain. I don't need to.

I blink back sharp tears. We walk. Our hands are locked together.

"What about you?" I say. "What's it like where you live? Where *do* you live?"

His eyes are amused, as if he knows this great joke and has been dying for me to ask. "Not far from you," he says.

"Do you . . . you don't sleep in the park, do you?"

"No," he says, stopping there, pulling me to him, his face an inch from mine, his breath sweet, the brim of his hat over both our heads. "Do you want me to? We could camp out together, Deirdre. . . ."

I laugh.

We walk. He says good-bye at the park. Stretches and yawns.

"Guess I'll be going to sleep now."

I walk on to school, and the morning's colored with ecstasy now, joy in every tree.

Liz Haddonfield and Claire Wright are no longer twins. Wright's hair is now short, in that obnoxious multitiered mushroom cut, puffy on top, tapering to a shaved-around-the-neck look. The SWAGs in chemistry class are putting on an amazing demonstration of the human ability to lie.

"It's fly!"

"It's virtual."

"It's sky."

"It's noble."

"You should do it, Liz. It'd look so cute on you."

"Well, I just might."

At lunchtime, passing the lockers, Ms. Mushroom Cut is standing before her boyfriend with her hands on her hips.

"You wanted the truth," Steve tells her. He has sort of a mushroom cut himself. It's spreading like a fungus through the SWAs. "And I'm saying it. I liked your long hair. Your face isn't right for that cut. You need a face like . . ."

He catches sight of me. "That girl. She'd look good in a short cut."

"You mean *that* voodoo witch?" She looks as if she's going to spit at me.

"She's kind of cute." He's enjoying torturing her.

"You scumbag," she tells him, huffing off so fast she makes a breeze by my face. I give the SWA a quick smile and he gives me a shrug and then slams his locker shut. A couple of other SWAs take the slam as a signal and I retreat out the doors to a whole chorus of slams.

At gym, the SWAGs are feisty, trying to bang into me, taking whacks at my leg with their hockey sticks. But I'm too quick.

When it's time to hit the showers, I suddenly

want to strip in front of them. I want to walk white and thin and naked and flat, like a ghost, past them into the shower.

I open my locker, look at them while they're talking. I feel just a twinge of fear, but it makes me feel better to look at them. I'm glad Ms. Brightley's prowling around, because I wouldn't be real happy if the SWAGs took my clothes.

"I can't believe he likes that Voodoo," Haddonfield's saying. Then she narrows her eyes at me. "Yeah, *you,* Voodoo."

"Me?" I say, pointing to myself. I take a few steps toward them. "You mean little old me?" A few more steps. They're backing up a little, looking at each other, laughing nervously. "Why, I wouldn't steal a boy. I nevah! I jest couldn't! I wouldn't know what to do! Unless, of course"—I drop the fake Southern ooze—"unless I had some"—I point all my fingers at them like claws—*"needles!"*

It's probably the best thing I've ever done in my life. The speech, the manic grin on my face; making them jump with my needle fingers. Doesn't matter that they think I'm a madwoman. I don't care, I don't care, I don't care.

I'm as exhilarated as if I just got offstage after performing at Madison Square Garden. I need that shower bad, and I throw off my clothes and just go and soak my skin.

I am brilliant and bad.

Now I'll tell you what really happened.

They did hit my legs with their sticks. I did not go into a Southern psycho act. I ignored them. I *did* get undressed and walk naked to the showers. I was calm. They did not steal my clothes. I was not brilliant and bad. I was good. And that's a start.

I see him every day. The time between our meetings—nights, days at school—is just filler. Dead time. My dreams at night are intense. His hands on me, his mouth, his scent, my body locked with his. Sometimes, in my dreams, he only looks. Doesn't touch. And wanting him, reaching for him, I ask him: *When?* And he always says: *We'll know.*

In real life, we haven't kissed. Sometimes, sitting with him in the boat, or when he stops in the woods and just holds my face and looks at me, I almost lean forward and kiss him. But there's still this fear of shattering all that is so good and powerful between us, so I do nothing but touch the dark silk of his hair where it falls into the curve of his cheek. And I stare. Strange things happen when we look into each other's eyes. Sometimes I feel as if he's inside me and I'm inside him and we're looking out at each other;

or we're becoming one person altogether. Sometimes I feel like we're not even people but aliens or spirits.

"The bayou's fed by the Atchafalaya River," he tells me as we drift one afternoon. Atchafalaya. With his slow, low voice, warm with secrets, a geography lesson is like making out.

The current suddenly picks up and tugs the boat, sending us spinning in the opposite direction. Johnny digs in with the oars and rows against the current, taking us through a narrow bend by an open bank, down a long stretch of water where we can drift some more. The bayou's full of bends and offshoots. It's easy to get lost if you don't know where you're going. Time's suspended and we glide through a dream world of a thousand magical things, every bright bird and twisted tree made more alive by what I feel for Johnny. We slide by stretches of pale purple water flowers, their color suddenly deepening as a cloud passes over the sun and then brightening as it passes away again. Everywhere you look there are rippling, subtle hallucinations, like magician's tricks.

Johnny's helping me grow familiar with all the changes. "Check it out, Deirdre," he says. "The current just shifted again." He rows hard and we escape along another narrow twist of green water banked by thick, mossy trees. The water's a green mirror, the trees reflected in waving images. I feel like Cleopatra slipping down the Nile.

This part gets so narrow, there's only a few feet on either side of our boat, and then it widens. A beachy, rocky area juts out with pelicans playing at the edge.

I laugh.

"Beautiful," he says.

"Yeah, they're great."

"I mean your laughter."

"Oh."

"You're so shy," he says.

"Yeah, right," I say, but I turn away.

He pulls the boat up to the rocky area, not too near because he doesn't want to frighten the birds. He tells me that the area wasn't even there a year ago; it was covered in water. He's always showing me dry spots that had water, watery spots that were once land.

"It goes in cycles," he tells me. "Gentle waters and then—*bam*—a bad wind comes up and everything gets stirred up and turned inside out. Death, disaster, crazy catastrophe. And then you wake up one day and it's mild again, safe to take your girl out with the boat."

He's telling me I'm his girl. It's the sort of expression that would have made me puke if I heard it back in the city from any of the guys I knew. But coming from him it's sexy. The words like a hand squeezing my stomach.

"Everything's in cycles," he's saying, watching me with his still face, intense eyes. "Change is constant. Do you know that?"

"I guess," I say. "Nothing lasts."

"But love," he says, looking deeper, so deep I feel I'm being hypnotized. I'm going to fall into his eyes. "It lasts. It can change you overnight into someone new."

He's leaning forward, our knees touching, his hand sliding down the side of my face, my neck, gently, the softest touch. . . . "It's always with you—like an invisible sword, an angel. . . ."

I reach for him, matching his gentleness, touching his cheek; we're so close, inches apart. His finger traces my mouth. I touch the top of his curved lip. I'm shaking, feel tears coming to my eyes. His breath is audible, like he's been softly crying. His finger slips into my mouth, mine into his. His hat falls forward down near his eyes, my hair falls in my face, our foreheads are touching, our fingers in each other's mouths, babies together for a crashing moment. And then we pull back staring, wild, and our hands are grabbing each other and our mouths come together. But it's just a kiss. A brush of our mouths and we pull back again, shocked. Love and danger dance crazy around us, spreading into the screeches of the birds in the air.

We're looking at each other, breathless, like people who've been fighting. He touches my mouth again, says, "Shhh." And then: "I love to kiss you. You're so beautiful to kiss. But not now."

"Okay." My voice is strange with a new huskiness.

"I want you to meet me tonight."

"Okay." Anything. Anywhere. You're torturing me.

"We'll come out here," he says. "We'll come out here, baby, with the boat, under the full moon." Okay. Yes. Yes. Yes.

Chapter 7

The smell hits you same time as the music. Burned onions and garlic and tomatoes mixed with that ancient group, the Grateful Dead, blasting away.

Curtis is in the kitchen with a glass of bourbon in one hand, the other tossing around sizzling meatballs with a big wooden fork in a black cast-iron pot. It's his standard dish—those greasy meatballs nearly green with oregano and basil and packed with coarsely chopped onions. Steam's rising out of a silver pot bubbling with his homemade tomato sauce—tons of tomato paste, more huge chunks of onion and garlic, fresh tomatoes, and a chopped-up carrot to sweeten the sauce. (He learned this trick from one of his models, an Italian girl.) Mom would never eat when he made his sauce with a carrot, but he always served it up to her, piling her plate with as many carrot slices as he could fish out—the creep—along with big crunchy pieces of Italian bread smothered with garlic. Mom always grabbed a yogurt those nights and ate in her room. And I always felt like a traitor dipping my garlic bread into Curtis's sauce.

He's got a tray of that garlic bread now, balanced on the toaster because every bit of counter and table space is covered with sauce, half-sliced onions, spilled jars of herbs, bowls still shiny with raw egg slime and meat remnants.

He looks like some crazy bum off the street, with that wild hair flying. His skinny hips in baggy jeans jerk around to the music. His old linty mustard-colored sweater looks like something from a dog's bed.

"Hey, kid," he says, gesturing hello with his fork. "Give us a hand, will ya?"

"I've got homework."

"Why don't you clear that junk off the table," he says. "And set it."

"I've got homework!"

Curtis looks at me, calm and cool, nodding his head to the beat, whistling along a little. "Set the table for four, and then make a salad, Dee."

It's almost six. And I'm supposed to meet Johnny at seven-thirty. I've got to be cool. Not attract attention.

"Doesn't Kenny have to help?" The words just pop out. Curtis whirls around. Now he's got that killer casual look, still whistling but a dangerous glint in his eyes.

"Deal with the table."

I can't help it. I just stand there, arms crossed, glaring.

Again: "Set the table." I don't move.

"Which word don't you understand?"

I don't want any big fights. I don't want him running after me. Not tonight.

I get busy with the table. Curtis bellows up the stairs: "Get your ass down here, Kenny!"

Dinner could have gone two ways: Curtis glowering and broody, hunched over his food.

Or Curtis all charming and twinkly, making special intimate jokes with each one of us, all merry merry with his bourbon and the spaghetti sauce on his sweater, happily clattering plates, heaping more servings whether you wanted them or not. Perhaps lifting himself from the chair briefly near the end of the meal to let out a fart, to be followed by more hearty laughter, and wet kissy smacks of his lips against Ms. Y.'s cheek. Ms. Y. perhaps whipping him across the upper arm with her limp, spaghetti-stained napkin.

In fact, it goes like this:

Curtis adds ice and water to his bourbon. Compliments me on the table and Kenny on the gourmet salad (Kenny's got that Betty Homemaker stuff lurking around in his genes), throwing in just a touch of sarcasm about how he had to threaten to break our wrists to get us to do it.

Kenny and I roll eyes at each other, pass and swallow the food. Robyn is the loudest thing at the table. She looks like a spotted albino vampire dressed for Valentine's Day, with her white hair, bright red lips, and red dress turning her face paler than usual. Her liverish freckles stand out nearly green.

She's leaving big red lipstick marks on her wineglass. "This Eye-talian sauce, honey, is so, now don't take it wrong, but it's so thick-like!"

Curtis beams at her. "Good stuff, huh." It's not a question.

"Oh, heh, heh, heh," Robyn says. "It surely is." I see her pushing it around her plate, picking out all the big onion and pepper chunks, making piles of her discards.

Curtis gives me a big wink as if we're pals. I grab up my plate.

"Where you running to, kid?" he says.

"Homework," I say. "Thanks for dinner."

It's seven-twenty. They're getting ready to leave and Robyn's been in the bathroom forever. I've just changed my shirt and then changed back again.

80

Don't want Curtis to notice. More than that, I don't want Johnny to notice. I don't want him to think I've been staring in the mirror, going crazy waiting, out of my mind with excitement.

I'm sitting at my desk drumming my fingers on my unopened science book. Come on. Go. Go. Get out. Get lost. Hurry. There's a rap at my door. "Yeah?"

Curtis slams it open. Slouches in the doorway. There's something about the way he's standing there, stooped, but still so tall his head almost reaches the top of the door, that reminds me of the old days when he'd yell at me and then we'd have a talk and a hug.

"Sure you don't want to come? It'll be good for your head. Get out of the house, go down-town . . ."

"Nah, I've got a lot of work to do," I say, opening up the book, shuffling papers around.

Curtis shrugs. "Hey, I can relate. I've been push-ing it to the limit all week." He's been loading up the van every day, taking his angel-whore paintings over to a jazz club called the Nubian Beat. They're going to hang a show for him. "If you'd rather hit the books than see your old man get his moment of glory . . ."

"Come on, Curtis," I say, starting to feel the guilt creeping in.

"She's snowing you, sugar." Ms. Thing is in the doorway. "She's got herself a sweetheart and she's sneaking off to see him."

Curtis lets out a sputter of laughter. "You sneaking off tonight, babe?"

"Oh, yeah," I say. "That's exactly what I'm doing."

Robyn goes and sits on my bed as if she's planning to stay forever. I can't stand that she's in my room. Even my mom used to ask before she came in.

Curtis makes himself comfortable next to her. I've got like three minutes. Get out. Go. Move.

I start looking up things I already know and writing them down in a nice orderly fashion.

Curtis claps his hands. "Well, that's it, let's move it."

"Sweetie," Robyn says, "it's none of my business, but I really think you should talk to—"

"Get going, woman!" he says with a bear growl, pretending he's going to bite her. She squeals. Disgusting. He pushes her out the door and says to me:

"Deirdre, there's no guy, right?"

I look up from my books, blinking and stunned. "No, Curtis."

"Just checking," he says. He leaves, then quickly ducks his head back in. "But if there is a guy, I want to meet him. And no running around at night until I do. And don't lie to me. Just don't ever lie to me, kid."

"Okay," I say. Back to turning pages, scanning for words. Willing him out. I feel his quick pat on my head before he thunders down the stairs.

I creep down, watch through the window as they take off in his van. The taillights disappear up the street. I run into the kitchen, where Kenny's eating a bowl of ice cream. Sitcom kid with his comic-book looks.

"I'm going," I tell him, pulling on my jacket.

"Where?" He looks bored.

"To meet a friend. But you can't tell."

"Okay," he says. He's good. I love him. Poor kid.

"How'd you get out of going with Curtis?"

He breaks into a shy grin. "I told him I was going over to Dave's. I told him Dave's mother's coming to pick me up so we can study together."

I try to picture Dave, and I see him like all Kenny's friends from the past—big, healthy, sweet-faced, typical. Not too jock, not too wimped out, just in between.

"So when's she coming?"

Kenny shakes his head, still with the shy grin. "She's not!" He looks absolutely delighted. "There is no Dave!"

"Hold on a second," I say. There's one minute

until seven-thirty on our digital clock above the stove. "Don't you have a friend named Dave?"

"No," Kenny says. His voice is squeaky with laughter and I start laughing too. He can hardly get the words out. "I don't have"—I'm holding my stomach, bent over, and he's snorting like a pig, delirious, tears leaking out of his eyes—"I don't have"—another snort—"any friends."

He's still chortling and sniffing and I'm dead silent. Man. I thought the kid was so popular. I feel for him, but it's seven-thirty now. I can't bring him with me, even though I almost want to.

"Look, I've gotta go," I tell him. I put my hand on his shoulder and pull it back when he gives me a weird look. "I'm late. But are you going to be okay?"

"Yeah," he says. "What do you mean?"

"Nothing," I say. "I'll be back soon, anyway. I want to talk to you, Kenny, okay?"

"What for?" He narrows his eyes. Sniffs back the last of his giddy tears and gets all hidden and macho. "What's up?"

"Nothing," I say. "Nothing. I love you."

"Buggy."

I'm out of there, running down the hall and out the door to the moon.

*　*　*

84

It's right up there, round and yellow and low. There's a wet breeze with a chill in it blowing up from the woods and I know. I know and it instantly kills me.

It's a rule. The more excited you get—heart in your throat, body weak, almost seeing and tasting and feeling the thing you want—that's how you know you're not going to get it.

When you want something this bad it doesn't happen.

Only this time maybe it's not too late to get rid of the excitement. Fool around with fate: I didn't really mean it. I don't really *have* to see him. I'm just going for a little walk in the woods for the pure nature-girl fun of it and if I should happen to run into Johnny, well, it would be real nice.

And who am I fooling? The woods are silent. I can see okay, but it's shadowy and eerie and there's that utter stillness of no other human life. I creep along, hearing only the *slap-slap* of water, my feet cracking twigs.

He could be late.

I'm a calm person, I tell myself. I am so cool. I'm Jane. I'm Jane walking in the woods, tall and black and not excited. Nothing fazes me. Not that boy. Stupid accordion, stupid hat. Who is he anyway? I don't love him.

Yes I do. Our spot, the clearing with the fallen log.

I don't want to breathe. I don't want to feel the phony power of the sky or earth. I don't want to be beautiful again.

Of course, he could be coming. I've been here only minutes. I'm not too late. I have to wait.

I lie on my back, on the cold, mossy ground, sticks poking into me, the moon higher and clearer and white now against ragged black space up between the trees.

He's somewhere staring at that moon. It was tonight, wasn't it? You think those things. Maybe he's running here. Maybe he's dead. If he's dead I can talk to him. Close my eyes. Johnny, are you dead? And then to my mother: Is he? How come you didn't warn me, Mom? Such stupid thoughts.

The thing about that kind of excitement, the thing about it that I always wonder is, Do you get so extra nervous and happy and full of expectations because deep inside you know it's not going to happen? It's important to find that out. Because then next time you could just save yourself the excitement and start off disappointed. I'm just a brain inside a body. I can't stop thinking, even with the white hole of the moon turning into two white holes in the sky as I stare myself cross-eyed. I think and think and think until I roll over onto my stomach. Shove the sleeve of my jacket into my mouth and wail.

But I can't cry over some boy the way I cried for

my mom. Even if he called me baby and said he would meet me tonight and kiss me.

And then I curl up under that moon and weep for my mom. The world is so empty and I've never been so lost.

At home, the clock glows a red 10:10 in the dark of the kitchen. I creak up the sticky wooden stairs and see Kenny's light on under his door. I remember that quick love and concern for him I had earlier like it was some kind of warped dream.

Into bed with all my clothes on. Pull up the covers. The room is bright with the moon. Bright as a 7–Eleven. Listen for cars, steps, my name being whispered. It still might happen. Toss all night with the moon. Hear Curtis and Robyn laughing outside. Shredded dreams of Johnny. Him tapping my shoulder, reaching for me, explaining over and over why he didn't show, long, complicated explanations. Wake to sunlight, one blank instant before the big thunderclap of dread. He's gone.

Okay, it's like this. You meet this great guy and you don't want to give him your number so you take his. You find a pink Xeroxed flyer about a rave in your pocket and you tear off a corner and write the guy's number down and stick it back in your pocket. And then when you look for the number the next day you can't remember if you took it out of your jeans or left it there, but when you check your pocket it's gone, so you trash your whole room looking. You find all kinds of pink slips—a corner of a school notice sticking out beneath a stack of fashion magazines, a piece of junk mail in the garbage, an ad for an all-you-can-eat barbecue on your dresser—and pretty soon you're wondering if maybe it wasn't pink at all, maybe it was yellow.

And then you start searching through the whole house, places you never would have put the guy's number—in the bathroom closet, in your brother's stinking gym bag, in the telephone table drawer downstairs where your father shoves the monthly bills, in the pockets of jackets you haven't worn for weeks. And the one most lunatic thing you cannot stop yourself from doing—at least four times you do this—is to go back to that same pair of jeans and feel inside all the pockets.

Now picture this: There is no number. There never was a number. You never asked the guy if he had a phone, because you were too busy taking trips into his eyes and making plans about the moon. You never dreamed he might drop out of your life.

So there are no jeans to go back to. Only places. The woods. The water's edge. His boat is never there. The gates around the park. Never there. Even inside the park sometimes, ignoring the stares. And just like all those fake pink slips, I sometimes think I see him. Like that old lady, clear across the park, with a wide-brimmed black hat. An old lady gets my heart pumping, makes me run.

Chapter 8

I'm looking all the time now, expecting to see him where he'd never be. When I cross the street at lunchtime, I wonder if maybe he's slipping out of the Home Comfort store. When I eat my fish sandwich at the fast-food shack, I look because maybe his dear face will explode out of the crowds. On those long walks home from school I don't make New York appear anymore. I just see Johnny. He's coming out of houses, riding on a bike, feet sticking out from under a car he's tinkering with, sitting up on a wide branch of a tree.

In the lumberyard with Curtis on Saturday, I'm hoping to see him step out from behind a propped-up board. Just stare at that board and maybe the wanting and the need will make him appear. Crazy.

Where the hell are you? What did I do? Are you

dead? What's keeping you from me? Be with me. Come back.

I never knew I had a mind like a video camera. I can play back every scene in close-up detail. *You're so beautiful to kiss. Love . . . it's always with you.* Pelicans. Handing me the flower. Our hug on the street in front of my house that morning. And his smell: woodsy, fresh, dark. You could never get that on tape. But I have it in the folds of my black sweatshirt. I go to put it on this afternoon because I'm chilly after school and it ambushes me. I don't want to waste it by wearing it, mix it up with my smell. I curl up on my bed with my shirt, breathing it in, bringing back his slow touch, the love in his eyes. Then I put it under my pillow. I'll just breathe it in when I need it.

How did we ever talk about so little? If I had it to do over I'd wipe away some of that mystery, trade it in for hard facts. Where do you live? Who do you live with? How do you get by? What's your favorite movie? What do you eat? What's the tragedy of your life? Do you have, for example, a pet? Do you ever pray? How, if the need should ever arise, would a

91

person find you if they were feeling totally desperate and abandoned and you'd just dropped off the earth?

Maybe he is worse than voodoo. Maybe he's the devil, put here to torture me.

This is how crazy I am: I'm sure he's not dead, because I'm positive that if he died he'd find some way to let me know. This is how crazy I am: It's been only four days since I've seen him and I feel as if it's been years. This is how crazy I am: I go shopping with Tanya and Aurora at the drugstore after school today. I steal a purple lipstick I will never use. I promise Tanya I will call her later with some notes from class so we can study on the phone. As if I ever would. This is how crazy I am: I tell Curtis about Johnny.

It's a Sunday night, school night. Curtis is in a great mood, singing, just out of the shower with his hair combed straight back as if he thinks he's completely hot. He looks like Jack Nicholson with his receding hair and big stomach and weird eyebrows.

I'm at the sink, washing dishes. Kenny's squirreled up in his room.

Curtis sings himself into the kitchen, grabs a clean dish from my hand and starts drying it.

"We're going out."

"You and Robyn?"

"No, me and you, kid."

"What?"

He grabs another dish. "You haven't seen my show, and I'm going to take you over there tonight. It's a whole little scene, music, poets. You'll dig it."

The last place I want to go is the Nubian Beat. We've passed it in the daytime and it looks like a falling-down shack from the outside, with a little blue neon sign.

"Look," Curtis says. "If you don't want to see my show—I mean, do you?"

I can tell he really wants me to see his paintings. He slouches with a plate in his big hands and a sort of shyness in his blue eyes. I try to picture us getting into his van, driving over, drinking Cokes and squinting around at his paintings. Then it hits me: Somewhere in that darkness, maybe Johnny'll be there. I'm not going to see him sitting at home with Kenny.

"What about Kenny?"

"Ask him," Curtis says. "Hey." He gives me a quick elbow in my side, and a wink. "I'm glad you're coming, Dee."

"Yeah?" Kenny's voice sounds young and shocked when I knock on his door. I open the door and he's lying on his stomach on his bed, reading.

"You want to go out?"

"What?"

He scrambles to a sitting position. There's a red mark on his cheek where his hand was pressed. I can't help it: That red mark makes me feel like hitting him. And his ultraclean room! Not just clean, but scary. The only thing on the floor is the weight equipment and a shiny red trash can, recently emptied.

On top of his tall white bookcase, there's a model of a dinosaur skeleton next to a slightly larger, realistic-looking iguana. On the shelves, every book is in place according to size. Kenny's floor is clean and softly shining; the bedcovers are all tucked in and smooth except for the part where he was lying. Pencils and pens are lined up next to perfectly stacked homework and schoolbooks on his desk. It looks like a nurse's room.

Okay, maybe I don't feel like hitting him. I feel like shaking him. Shaking him out of the locked-up, neatly packaged, good-boy loneliness of his life. Actually, I just feel like splitting. I don't want to see his face all upturned and expectant, eyes dreamy from reading. I don't want to remember that he doesn't have any friends. And I don't want to convince him to come with us, because I don't want him to come. Even though he probably should. And if I were a good sister I would. Man.

"We're going out," I say. "We're going to see Curtis's show at the Nubian Beat." Kenny starts putting on his shoes.

"Supposed to be music and poetry and stuff," I say with disgust. "He wants to know if you want to come."

"Should I go?" How can you hate and love your brother at the same time? He's got that sweet, Kenny-as-a-baby look in his eyes that he had when he used to follow me everywhere and ask me a thousand questions. But when a big kid like Kenny needs you, it's not cute anymore.

"I wouldn't," I say. "I mean, go if you want, but the only reason I'm going is Curtis is practically forcing me."

He kicks off his shoes and falls back on the bed. Picks up the book again, looks over at me. "So I don't have to go, then?"

"Nah," I say. And then: "Unless you want to." And then, because I feel like I tricked him or something, and I can't stand the idea of him lying on his bed reading all night while we go off, I say: "Are you sure you don't want to?"

"Yeah." And then he shoots me the nicest smile. "Thanks." Yeah, for everything.

People stand outside the Nubian, faces lit in the slow blue blink of the neon sign. Their cigarette smoke's caught in the light of an old-fashioned streetlamp on the corner. The sidewalk thrums with a deep drumbeat that goes up your feet and echoes in your chest.

There's only one kid around here, and that's this short-haired boy who for one instant reminds me of Johnny. He's got the same warm biscuit-colored skin, a Creole look. He's leaning against a boarded-up window, smoking a clove cigarette. That sweet crab apple–smelling smoke brings me back too. The hippies used to smoke them in the school bathrooms a few years back, when everyone was wearing rainbow hair wraps and talking about Woodstock.

My mind's always scrambling to make things familiar: That guy almost looks like Johnny. Or, Gee, I know that smell. Maybe this is home, Toto.

A light-skinned fat guy in a suit claps his hand on Curtis's back. "Hey, it's the man."

I could kill myself for talking Kenny out of coming. If Kenny were here we could be like two kiddies out with their dad. I wouldn't feel so much like Curtis's date.

One of the last times I went out with Curtis was two years ago in the East Village. We went into this tiny little Irish club. There was room for only twelve people and Curtis seemed to know all of them. A girl was strumming a guitar and singing a horrible song. Curtis put his arm over my shoulder and introduced me to all these weird older people. They looked like ancient rock stars. He told some of them I was his date. He told me I made him look good.

"Get off the merchandise, buddy." The fat man is shouting at a purple-haired drunk who's climbing all over a pearl-gray BMW. That's when I realize I know the fat man. Jane's dad.

"Watch the wheels," he says to the drunk. Jane's dad drapes his arm across Curtis's shoulders. He opens the club door and looks back at me to wink. Louder drumming and homey cooking smells pour out the door.

"She's a sweetheart," he says to Curtis.

"She's my kid," Curtis says. Good.

"You don't say." Jane's dad pauses in the doorway. "That's a beautiful thing." He gives me a warm look. "You come on in and be at home."

Everything leads to the raised stage in the back. There are tables covered with white paper and booths stuffed with people laughing and sipping coffee. The place smells like espresso and some kind of exotic, spicy cooking, the sizzle of garlic and peppers from

97

behind a swinging kitchen door. Waitresses bring around drinks, but it doesn't feel like a booze place. Jane's standing by a big silver cappuccino maker in a corner, hissing out some foamy white cream into a cup. She takes me in, gives me a nod. I nod back.

The Nubian has a rosy glow coming from the tall standing lamps with peachy satin shades and swingy tassels. And every wall's covered with the big sweet-faced whores Curtis painted. They make the place look like a Paris café. The biggest one of all, a lipstick-smeared Robyn with her white hair around her head like a halo, is high up on the wall behind the stage. She's sailing in an aqua sky in her red lacy underwear. I'd rather look at the players: three guys with drums between their knees and a girl smacking a tambourine against her hip.

We grab a tiny table off to the left of the stage just big enough for two. A whole gang of Curtis's fans push tables together and pull up chairs. Everybody likes Curtis.

Curtis is beaming. He shoots a nervous look at me to see if I notice this adoration and then he's ordering whiskey for everyone and hitting the table with his hand in time to the beat.

I miss Johnny. I check the door every time it swings open. Some girl starts doing poetry, new spoken-word stuff in time to the music, stamping her feet, swinging her hair around, snapping her fingers.

Everyone is snapping their fingers, snapping and clapping like a thousand clams clicking their shells together. Everyone but me and Jane, who's sitting on the far side of the room sipping coffee, tall and cool and bored.

I think she's forgotten about me, but when I sneak a little toss of Curtis's whiskey into my coffee I see her look at me. Just a quick movement of her eyes, but she lets me know that she not only sees but thinks it's stupid.

It's quiet outside when we leave. We get into the van and Curtis, still warm and chuckling, comes out with:

"Who is he?"

"Huh?"

"You heard me." He's not unfriendly. Turning the key in the ignition but not taking off.

"That was a pretty cool place, Curtis."

"What's his name?"

When Curtis knows something, he knows.

"Johnny."

"Good girl." He pulls out.

Two blocks down: "And you love him?"

"Jesus, Curtis. Why don't we talk about your paintings?"

"You weren't studying my paintings in there," he

says. "Maybe you admired them for a second—who could blame you? Hot stuff, huh?"

I nod. "Yeah, they looked good."

"You were a million miles away. Even with that little nip."

"I didn't . . . I—"

"Save it, kid. So do you? You love him?"

I turn my whole face toward the window. See nothing in the black but my eyes. "Could you just leave me alone?"

"And he took off. Poor kid. But you gotta get tough."

I say nothing.

"Unless you want to get good and obsessed. I mean, sometimes that leads you somewhere."

I want to know where it can lead. He knows that I know that he knows what he's talking about. But I don't want to beg the enemy for information.

"I guess you are pretty tough," he says. Gives me a light punch in the arm.

"Ow." I look at his grinning profile.

"Destiny," he says. That's my mother's name. "Do you know how many Destinys there are in the Peekskill telephone book?"

Peekskill was where he met Mom. She lived there and was an actress. She starred in a town play when she was only sixteen.

"I knew she lived on her own," Curtis says. "She

100

told me that when I brought her the roses." He loved her so much in the play that he ran out during the second act and bought her a dozen purple roses and brought them backstage.

"But she didn't give me her number. She went off with some blond jock on a Yamaha. So I stayed overnight in some fleabag. I spent the night with the Peekskill phone book, looking up her number by her first name."

"How'd you do that?" I'd never heard this part of the story.

"Easy. Fifteen pages of the letter *A*. No Destiny. Twenty-two pages of the letter *B*. No Destiny. Then skipping around, the *Z*'s—they were short—and then the *L*'s. Actually the *O*'s and the *M*'s first; I had a feeling she was Irish and I'd find her under *O'* something or *Mac* something. She had those earnest, clear blue eyes and those great legs."

"So how'd you find her?"

"Not in the book. I found her the next morning at the bus station. She was standing there with a suitcase, ready to leave town. She had some plan to go to Cleveland to look up an old aunt to try to get some money to get a ticket out to Hollywood."

"Are you serious?"

"As a heart attack. So I told her I'd give her the money but she had to drive to Manhattan with me and I'd hand it straight over to her. I just convinced her of the whole deal with my charm and sincerity."

Curtis is whistling, pleased with himself. Story over.

"And then did you?"

"Did I what?" Slightly annoyed. We're turning onto our street.

"Did you give her the money?"

"What do you think?" he says. "Come on, kid, you know the rest. We got married, had you. End of story, morning glory."

"Oh, right." Except for the mystery part when he got nasty and distant and nothing was ever the same in our house and she ended up dying.

"And you know how this applies to you? You and your man, John?"

"No, Curtis, why don't you tell me."

We pull up into the lot behind our house. He lets the engine idle, flicks on the interior light so I have to see his face. "What it all boils down to is this— he'll be back. You'll see him again. Only . . ."

He shakes his head, blows air out of his mouth— *pppfff*—as if he's blown away by something, disappointed.

"Only what?"

"Only I'm going to meet him when he shows. Got it?" He points a thumb and index finger at me like a gun.

"Sure." I bang my door open. "Thanks for to-night," I say. Running now in the night air, grass wet through my shoes. "Gotta get up early, going straight to bed."

I look back. He's still sitting in his seat with the seat belt on. Blinks the car headlights at me and gives me the thumbs-up sign.

It's been a weird night. And the weirdest thing is, before I fall asleep I think I feel Mom's hand on my head. Maybe I'm concentrating so hard, I just squeezed it out of my imagination. The feeling is almost there: her cool hand on my head.

I slip my hand under my pillow and pull out the black sweatshirt and breathe in. His scent is gone. And I'm too tired to leap up and find the Charmette phone book and look up Vouchamps. Or Voodoo. Or just plain Johnny, starting with the *A*'s.

Chapter 9

We're outside doing laps for gym, our fourth time around. It hits me that just a few yards away, pressed up against the chain-link fence, is Johnny.

You only get what comes to you when it wants to come to you. You only get it when you don't want it or care about it too much. I don't know why they don't teach you these rules from day one, starting in preschool.

I can't put together the fact of Johnny standing there with the week of wanting to see him. I run right past him.

"Showers," Ms. Brightley yells, and we fall out of line, huffing, wiping sweat off our faces. I sneak a look.

He looks different. Weird. That's it, no hat. His head looks strange. He's skinnier. And no accordion. Fingers curled around the chain-link fence staring at me like some kind of stalker. A few of the girls nudge

104

each other and point, shooting me looks. Brightley's walking off to the locker room, so at least she doesn't notice.

I'm pissed.

Anger is the one thing I haven't felt this whole week of missing him, and here it is. It's like, I guess he isn't dead after all, so what kind of reason did he have for not showing?

I have this urge to ignore him, disown him, walk away.

"Hey," he calls. I look back once, but keep going.

"Deirdre!"

I'm deaf.

But after I shower and get dressed and grab my stuff, I'm feeling twitches in my stomach. Maybe I should just see him. Yes. No.

"God, that guy is spooky," Tanya says. That alone makes me want to see him.

I go out the double doors into the gray afternoon and down the steps. I'm not looking. I am not looking. Kids spill out, loud around me.

"Hey, Deirdre. Deirdre." He's out in front, with everyone staring at him. He's on one side of the fence, so I start walking the other way, around the school toward the back entrance. He follows around the fence. Everyone is looking. I walk the other way; he walks the other way; we're walking together now, the fence between us.

"Stop for a second," he says. "Stop and let me come around."

"Go to hell."

"Honey," he says. "Look at me."

"Screw you."

"Baby," he says. "I have to talk to you. I have to tell you what happened."

I stop, face him through the fence. Dimly aware of kids all around watching. And then all I know is this beautiful face I've missed. The same sweet darkness of his eyes, hopeful, begging. A twitch around his beautiful mouth. We could be laughing again. Holding hands. Kissing. He loves me.

"I've missed you so much," he says. "Baby, I'm so sorry."

My throat closes and I feel the sting behind my eyes. I keep walking.

"Oh, man," he says, and then he takes off running. I head back behind the school toward the playground, where there are rusty swings and curled white petals dropping off magnolia trees.

He's running up behind me. Cheers and jeers from out on the sidewalk: "Yo, man, get her!" "Watch out, Johnny!"

His arms are around me. I feel the sudden weight and heat of him against me, smell his wild woodsy smell, like the fur of a silver wolf. He turns me around. I'm so limp I'm like liquid for a second and then I try to pull out of his arms. He's grabbing my hand and I'm pulling back hard but I don't want him to let go.

"You've got to listen to me," he says. "And then if you want to leave, okay, go. But don't go. I need you. Listen to me, I love you."

I stop pulling a little. He strokes my hand, raises it to his mouth, kisses it. "Did I hurt you?" His eyes are wet, sad. "I don't ever want to hurt you like that."

I feel the tears all crowding up in my throat.

"God, Deirdre. Deirdre, I'm sorry, forgive me. Do you forgive me?"

I shake my head. He steers me over to a low, rusty merry-go-round, out of sight of everyone.

The merry-go-round sags when he sits up close to me. He puts his arm around my shoulder. "Things have been real bad," he says, quiet, almost in a whisper. "It's my brother." I look at him. There's a long scratch running down his face by his ear. "Something happened, you've got to let me tell you about it. Don't pull away from me, Deirdre, you've got to listen. Okay. Okay, baby."

His hands stroke my hair. "It's going to be okay." His voice runs through me. "I won't ever do that again. I'm so sorry. Do you believe me? Do you?"

I'm nodding into his chest, my face pressed up against the roughness of his shirt. I can breathe him

107

in, live, in person. Then I pull back suddenly, my face wet, nose running. "Where's your accordion?"

He breaks into a low laugh and kisses my cheek.

"That's part of it," he tells me. "I left it like ransom so I could come get you."

We're on his boat under the low gray sky, so low it seems as if it's fallen into the water. Johnny's talking more than he ever has, telling me the strange facts of his life.

"On my daddy's side, my grandma was Native American, and my grandpa was Creole with French Canadian roots. My mom was a white mongrel, Irish, Italian, maybe some Swedish. My daddy played Cajun music with a band, the Hooters. He didn't make a lot of money, but enough to get by."

"What was he like?"

"He was okay," Johnny says. "He took me fishing once. He liked to play hide-and-seek sometimes and I'd go up in a tree and he'd pretend he didn't know I was up there. He was a good dad."

"What about your mom?"

His eyes flick away. "I don't know. She was okay. Drank a lot."

His parents died in a car accident when he was five. They were old, his father sixty, his mother forty-five. The only things they left behind were two boxes of *National Geographic*s and a couple of accordions. Johnny and his big brother, Leander, were raised by their mother's mother in her big yellow house in downtown Charmette near the school, until the old lady died when Johnny was seven.

"Leander's twelve years older than me," Johnny says. He has this look in his eyes. He says Leander's name soft, as if it's a miracle. As if Leander's a saint.

They stayed in the big yellow house for a while and no one messed with them or tried to put Johnny in a foster home. They were county dependents, living on welfare and food stamps.

When Johnny was thirteen Leander tried to kill himself, and the authorities tried to put him in a hospital but he ran away. He left behind more suicide notes, so everyone in town thought he really did it this time, drowned in the bayou.

The tax people took the yellow house away and they tried to stick Johnny in an orphanage, but he was too quick for them and they were scared of him. "Because," he tells me, head cocked charmingly to the side, and with a flash of his white teeth, "I was not a natural child."

Johnny was on his own after Leander went away.

"But you were thirteen!" I say. I sit up straight in the boat. "Johnny, you were a little kid." I lean forward, wanting to touch him, but he seems too far away. "How'd you do it?"

"I had my ways," he says. "Still do."

I feel as if he's been storing his life up in his head like a secret.

He brushes a strand of hair off my cheek. "Don't be so worried. Leander was there half the time, too, when he wasn't loony. He'd come back and force me to read all these library books: Dostoyevsky's *Crime and Punishment;* H. G. Wells's *Outline of History;* and Emily Post's book of etiquette."

He's silent as he rows us past the spot where we saw the pelicans and makes a quick dip to the right and then the left, a way we've never gone, and then he leans back and sighs.

"I have a house," he says. "A cabin, anyway."

I stare at him.

"I wanted to bring you there before, Deirdre," he says. He's steering the tip of the boat up close to a stump sticking out of the water. It's got a hook and a heavy cord and he runs the cord through a hook on the rowboat and ties it. I feel a thrill of fear. There's no house in sight. Just marsh and weeds running up to the edge of thick, dark woods.

"But, Leander, he sometimes shows up like a ghost and I didn't want you to be scared. But he's

110

okay now. He's there and you're going to meet him. It's going to be okay."

In the green afternoon light, we move through a barely marked path. There's a sudden clearing and the cabin appears. It's made of dirty-blond logs and there's a stone chimney on top, two windows facing us and a heavy door standing wide open. Leaking out is the sound of *The Price Is Right.*

Inside it's surprisingly big, with high beamed ceiling and rafters made of whole logs. The air is hot and stuffy, like Thanksgiving on a warm November day. Instead of turkey, there's the smell of something burning—kind of like pot, but with a medicinal smell—and there's a trail of cellophane cupcake wrappers leading from the door to the couch, where a girl sits with her back to us watching the game show on a battery-operated *Dick Tracy*–size TV propped up on a table in front of her.

She is wearing Johnny's hat and has done something complicated with her long, black hair. Half of it lies loose below her shoulders, shiny against her apricot-colored silky robe. The other half is clasped in loosely rolled pink rubber curlers. As I stand in the doorway one of her hands shoots out and drops another cupcake wrapper on the floor. The other hand lifts and droops at the wrist, the fingers fluttering in

111

an elegant movie-star wave. All of this without turning around. I would happily kill her.

"Oh, man," Johnny says, grabbing up the wrappers to his chest, dropping some because there's so many of them. "Hey, Deirdre, sit, sit." He gives me a helpless little-kid grin, juts his head in the direction of a low bed covered with a bright Navaho blanket. "You knew I was having a guest," he says to the girl. His tone is indulgent, almost affectionate, beneath the scolding. "You could've kept the place nice."

"You might say thank you before you start in complaining," says the girl, slowly turning her head around, taking me in briefly before focusing all her attention on Johnny. "Some people would be infinitely appreciative of my work." Her voice is like a queen's, royal and deep. And I can see now the one most spectacular thing about her, besides her voice and her junk-food appetite. She is not a she.

He looks at me again, flicks his eyes away as if I'm not even close to the guest he expected, goes back to addressing Johnny. He's got Johnny's face, years older, with smeared lipstick on his mouth and heavy eye makeup and orange foundation that cakes into the deep lines around his mouth. If you can picture that. It's almost too much for me and I'm sitting right there.

"Some people would be delighted," he's saying, "to have a direct path by which to find me."

"Okay, I've found you," Johnny says, dumping the wrappers into a garbage bag. "Good work, Hansel."

"I prefer Gretel," says the noble creature on the couch, with a quick rise of his thin, plucked brows. "If you don't mind. If it's not too much of an effort."

Johnny messes around with a raging-hot wood stove, mutters something about the heat in the place, then plops down on the bed next to me. "Dierdre," he says, "this is my brother, Leander, Deirdre." Then to me in a stage whisper: "You can call him Lee."

Even above the game-show clatter, Leander catches the whisper. "She certainly may not!" he says. He rolls his eyes at me in a murderous panic, like a racehorse about to be sent to the glue factory.

And after that he doesn't say another word to me, just: "Johnny, I'm craving a lemon ice . . ." and "Johnny, do you know the price of a new stove?" I hate the way he says *Johnny* with total ownership.

There's no ice in the house (lemon or otherwise). There's no electricity: Coleman lanterns hang from the rafters; tall red candles and kerosene lamps stand neatly lined up on a counter by the sink. At least he has a pump.

A skinny ladder near the couch area leads up to a loft. There's not much else in the house—a small bathroom, a kitchen table with chairs, a sanded-down tree stump for a coffee table next to the bed, with poetry books and newspapers tossed on it. The cabin has a good feeling.

Johnny leans back against some cushions and pats the spot next to him. I just sit stiffly on the edge of the bed. He's relaxed now, happy, at home. And I feel shy, as if we're strangers. The light grows dimmer in the cabin and the TV chatters on. No one makes a move to light a lamp. Soon Leander is snoring, his head resting on the back of the couch, his lipsticked mouth open. Johnny's hat falls off Leander's head and to the floor with a thud.

Johnny tiptoes around and peers into Leander's face. He lets out a sputter of laughter. "Deirdre, you've got to see this."

Leander's snoring away with his apricot robe open, legs sprawled apart. He's wearing blue jeans and a Mickey Mouse shirt under the robe. He's got each arm hugged around an accordion, as if they're two teddy bears.

Johnny slides one of the accordions out, the one I always see him with. Then he kind of scoots Leander down on the couch so his head's on a pillow and his feet are propped up on the armrest. He covers him with a blanket and leaves the other accordion on his stomach with his arm over it. As a finishing touch, he puts his hat near Leander's head.

"Just in case," he tells me. "He won't be up for a day, because he hasn't slept in three days. That's how he is when he gets like this—up and up and then down for the count."

I feel a sudden kinship with the poor tortured guy. All those nights when I couldn't sleep and days when I was exhausted—the energy and drain of missing Johnny. I feel like wiping off some of Leander's orange makeup and looking at his real face.

Johnny's tidying up a little as *I Love Lucy* plays on the TV. It's coming in sputtery as if the batteries are wearing out, but it gives a certain modern, hopeful feeling to the darkening cabin. If Ethel and Lucy can be plotting against Ricky, nothing truly sinister could be happening in the world. Or at least in this cabin.

I start to feel like myself again.

Next to the TV there's a tied bundle of thin gray sticks sitting in a heavy chrome ashtray. "Sage," Johnny tells me. "You burn it and it chases out the demons."

He lights a lantern and it fills the room with yellow light. He leaves the lantern on a table and I follow him up the sturdy ladder to the loft. "I'll tell you about Leander's demons," he says, as if he's promising me a bedtime story.

We lie on our stomachs on a thin mattress facing a

round window. It's even warmer up here. The sky is a gray-purple between the black tree branches scratching up against the window.

With Leander snoring downstairs and the TV still going, I feel as if we're two kids waiting for our mother to call us down for dinner. We can giggle and play but not be so loud we wake our monster father from his nap.

"My brother lives in New Orleans in a minicommune with four other guys," Johnny says. "When Leander starts getting really tough to live with they kick him out."

"And then he shows up at your place?"

Johnny nods. "He shows up or I have to go and get him. And when he sees me, all he wants me to do is play the accordion until my fingers bleed." Johnny shows me his open hand and even in the dim light I can make out cuts and calluses on the tips of his fingers.

I ask him if he plays Cajun-style the way his father did, that kind of jumpy, happy sound you hear coming out of bars and on the streets.

"Nah," he says. "I have my own way. My own way for Leander." Johnny started making up new sounds and rhythms on the accordion when they lived with their grandmother. The old lady hated his

116

playing, so he had to do it in the woods. They'd go out there and Leander would dance strange circle dances around Johnny.

"And that's the only time you play it—for Leander?" I feel a sharp little twirl of jealousy under my ribs.

"I play it for money, too," he says, not looking at me, as if he's guilty. "The next town over, I play it two nights a week on the streets. Food money."

"You play the same stuff you play for Leander?"

"Nah, I'm like an organ-grinder, churning out the stuff the tourists like."

"How come you don't play in Charmette?"

He turns onto his side, facing me. Strokes the side of my cheek with his rough finger, but gently, barely touching me. "So many questions," he says. "I've missed you so much."

I swallow. "So why don't you?"

He rolls onto his back, covers his eyes with his hands. "I don't want anyone knowing my business. Knowing me," he says. "Except you." He opens two fingers of his hand in a *V,* so his eye peeks out at me. "Do you like my cabin?"

"Yeah."

He rolls onto his side again, reaches out his arm, and starts massaging my neck. Every deep squeeze of his strong hands is like a shot through my body, but I keep on talking as if he's not touching me.

117

"How did you get this cabin?"

"My grandma was always talking about a little cabin in the woods she lived in as a girl. I was kind of psychic. I could feel things out, know things. When she died I took that boat and went exploring. We found the place. There's no road to it and no one knows about it. It was Leander's and my playhouse, and every time he's coming out of his skin he comes back here."

Again, that twist of jealousy when he uses that worshipful tone about his brother.

"How often does he come here?"

"I don't know. Four, five, sixteen times a year. Usually around the full moon. But not every month." He stops rubbing my shoulders. Leaves his hand resting on my back. "I'm sorry, baby, I should have told you. . . . I mean, I should have known that maybe on that night, that full-moon night, he might've showed."

I rest my head down on my crossed arms. "I guess you're not always psychic."

"I knew you'd be okay," he says, gently gliding his hand down and up my back, as if he's smoothing the fabric of my shirt. "Deep inside, you knew we'd be together soon. Didn't you? Leander needed me; I had to care for him. I hated to hurt you, but I came to you as soon as I could leave him. I knew you'd understand."

My body tenses. The thrills are blocked off and his hand is just a hand now.

"Oh, Deirdre," he says. "Don't get mad. I knew while I was away you'd feel how much I loved you; I knew it would keep us close."

That's twice he's said it to me, *I love you,* but I don't want to say it back to him. He's moving his hand again, circular, feathery touches, and my body's jumping inside again, eight million electric responses to his touch, wanting us to come together, to feel him, to kiss him, but there's a strange new tension between us.

Before, when I hardly knew him, when he wasn't fixed in my mind with a job and a house and a crazy brother, I trusted him more.

Now that I know all these things, it makes him feel less familiar somehow. It adds this element of danger. It's as if I'm hanging out with a whole new person. And when he moves closer and closer, a breath away from my face, to kiss me—I pull back as if I've been bit and I scramble to my knees and I'm halfway down the ladder when I hear his warm, forgiving laughter.

We've gathered up our stuff. Neither of us has said anything about the almost-kiss. Leander's still snoring and Johnny's talking in a whisper.

119

"I'll probably bring him back tomorrow," he says. "It's good to bring him back when he's doing okay. Don't want him moving in with me, do I?" He gives me a little jab in the side, his eyes all shiny, as if he's known all along how threatened I am by Leander.

"I don't know," I say. "He comes with his own TV and he likes your playing."

Johnny slings his accordion over his shoulder and then we're off. He takes a freshly lit lantern. It's nearly all dark and the moon's hidden behind clouds. I'm relieved to be in the fresh purple air outside the stuffiness of the cabin, but my heart pulls a little as we leave.

Chapter 10

Bats looking like animated black rags speed-flap in the sky. The air's warmer than before, as if it were a spring night instead of November.

We've been moving along the swamp in silence, the boat feeling like a tiny living room with the yellow kerosene lamp on the seat next to me and the accordion next to Johnny.

"How come you never play it for me?" I run my hand lightly across the instrument. The silvery folds are like a mirror, picking up swirling patterns of light from the lantern and a violet tint from the last light in the sky.

"Okay," he says, handing me the oars. "I'll play."

He's let me row a few times before, but I'm not sure how to navigate. "Don't worry," he says. "We'll just drift for a while. Just don't get us stuck up in the weeds."

He holds the accordion, looking at me as if he's

waiting for something. I say nothing. Usually I get weird when someone picks up an instrument and plays something for me. In New York there was a guy at school who had a guitar. I was sitting outside on the blacktop once eating my lunch and he just happened to be sitting near me and he whipped out his guitar and looked right at me while he sang this corny eighties song totally off-key. I almost died from humiliation. I never know what kind of look I'm supposed to have on my face when someone's singing to me. Are you supposed to have this intense, concentrating look or a slightly adoring look with your lips parted? And are you supposed to nod to the beat or clap your hands, or what?

The last time I remember feeling comfortable with someone playing just for me was probably when I was a little kid and my father strummed his guitar at family outings. I don't feel weird with Johnny, but then again, he hasn't started playing yet.

"Well," Johnny says. "What do you want to hear?"

"I thought you were just going to play your own style," I tell him. "Not the tourist stuff."

"Don't you know any songs?" he says patiently.

So I say the first thing that comes into my mind—" 'Puff, the Magic Dragon' "—and instantly feel like dying.

But Johnny leans forward and kisses my cheek.

"My darling," he says. Then a little nod to himself and—*wham*—he's into it.

The soupy air trembles with the moans of the instrument and I'm afraid the boat's going to tip with the frenetic motion of his elbows. It's as if he's breathing into the thing with his long fingers, making it sound like organ music. The notes blend and change so quickly, at first I can't pick out any tune. I'm glad for the dense twilight and the crazy shadows of the lamp, because my face is burning hot. He probably never heard the Puff song, or thought I was being sarcastic, but then something comes together in the shower and sparks of the notes and . . . he's playing it. I can pick out the tune but it's not coming out straight, it's being held up in these heartbreaking detours of sound and rhythm.

And then there's this other sound, climbing up into the song like a low vibration. He's humming and singing, in French and in English. It's so sad and sweet and beautiful, his singing and the aching, breathing noise of the accordion. The sounds break over me in waves.

Then something flashes in my eyes.

I see the yellow of the lamp jump up out of the water in two, no four, globes of light, bouncing out there on the black surface as if Johnny's music made the lamp come alive and form itself into round balls of light skimming on the water.

Johnny, not breaking the rhythm or the song, swivels his head to the lights and then turns back to me, grinning now, nodding his head, like, I know, I know, I see it too.

The lights are following the boat, about fifteen feet away. Then I see dark breaks in the water, shadowy bodies. The lights are alligator eyes. A mama and a baby. Oh, my God.

Johnny's playing for them now, a dragon song for the water dragons, and his singing turns to a clicking of his tongue and then a squeaky sound sucked in between his pursed lips, in time to the song, like air being let out of a balloon—and I realize he's calling these guys; he wants them near. My terror fades and I can relax into the song and the night. The great fearless lizards swim alongside our boat with their eyes resting on the water's surface like bubbles of incandescent gold.

Johnny's notes are slower now—low, heaving cries—and he's whistling, a sort of bird warble that almost has a visible spiral to it, starting high and then swirling around and sinking and then spinning up again. A deep jungle UFO sound. And then he's silent. Just a few beads of sweat on his forehead. And two sets of glowing eyes waiting and then swimming off. Man.

Johnny props his elbow on his knee and his chin in his hand and looks at me. "Don't you sing?"

"Did you want me to?" I say finally.

He shakes his head. "But I bet you whistle," he says. He takes the oars from me and propels us through a sharp snaky turn, heading toward my woods. It seems more silent than before, with just the slap of the oars in the water and my heart in my ears and his breathing and a sparse chirp of night frogs.

I used to do the loudest ear-splitting whistle for a taxi and I'd make my mother laugh every time and have the cabs coming to us like pigeons to old ladies. "Not anymore," I answer. "But Johnny, that was so beautiful." My hand flies to my mouth as if to keep the words back, because *beautiful* doesn't get near describing his music. Now I understand Leander. I can see how someone could go insane from needing to hear that music.

"Thank you," Johnny says. There's something so humble in the way he says it, in the quick lowering of his eyes. All the stuff I learned about him in the cabin, all the new sides to him, seem to fit now. I don't even feel jealous about his closeness to Leander. I forgive him for the week of not seeing me, because I see his heart. He's real. I love him.

It's so strange the way your shifting perceptions of someone—good, bad, and everything in between—can seem to change them when all along they're always the same person and you're the one seeing them differently.

Johnny puts the oars down and leans in close to me and I can't even take my hand from my mouth, so he takes it away and puts his mouth on mine and then we're kissing.

It starts as the sweetest kiss and then the sweetness spreads and explodes and there's danger in this kiss. He's on his knees in the boat pulling me toward him and there's no him and no me, just the kiss, until the boat bangs into something and the lantern sputters. We pull apart, dizzy, and can't take our hands off each other, holding on even as he takes a few swipes at the water with the oar, and then he stops rowing and grabs me again and our kiss this time is so melting and slow that we keep on kissing even when the boat bangs up against a bank and water sloshes and smacks up the sides.

After an eternity of kissing, just kissing, we finally pull away and he rows, neither of us daring to look at the other, our feelings thick between us, and he docks the boat at the edge of my woods and we run and trip and stumble to our spot. I lie with him in the clearing where he taught me how to breathe in the sky and the earth. We lie on our sides tangled up in each other, pressed against each other like twins, our mouths tasting each other in the warm, mossy, flowers-and-dirt-smelling, damp Louisiana night air. I feel as if we're still on the boat, gently rocking, floating in the dark, so safe and so wild together. He tells me he wants me, slides his hand up under my shirt, his hand on my back, the heat of his hand on my skin, the sharp intake of his breath—as if he's been wounded just by touching me . . . That sound—just that sound makes me want him so much it physically hurts. And I tell him no and he says it's okay, we'll know when it's right.

"You're just so beautiful, Deirdre," he tells me. "Do you feel it?" he asks, and I do feel it, our eyes on each other's faces, our eyes no longer eyes because we're not human anymore, we're things from each other's dreams, we're these powerful, magical beings so beyond normal human love that we're inside each other's cells and souls, like beautiful aliens.

"I love you," he whispers. "You're like my other half."

He says this just as I'm thinking I might bleed if they tore us apart. If we had to separate. Because even though we're not having sex, even though there are layers and layers of clothes between us, I feel so attached, we're like one. I want so badly to feel more of him, and then I flash on the phrase *make love*. I have always hated that expression until now. I hated all the terms for sex—*sleep together,* so nothing, like cardboard, and *fuck,* like something people who hate each other do. But Johnny and me—his quiet breathing, the look in his eyes, our fingers laced together—we're already making love without sex.

I've lost all track of time, but it comes back in a second.

Johnny props himself up on one elbow and says, "I want to take you back to my cabin." He brushes a sticky strand of hair from my cheek. "I've got to check on Leander and I don't want to leave you."

Oh, my God. I run my hands through my hair, which feels all wild and tangled. Smooth my shirt. My face tingles, my chin burns, my mouth feels bruised from our kisses.

"I can't. I've got to get home."

"Come on." He tugs my sleeve between two fingers like a little kid. "Come on, you can."

"No, Johnny."

So he walks me to my door with his arm across my shoulder. Amber living room lamps and blue and green TV flashes light up the windows on my block. My own house is half dark with no sound floating through the open, screened windows.

Please don't be home, Curtis. Let me get to my room, let me be alone. Please. It's like the only thing that would make leaving Johnny tolerable—if I knew

I could go straight to my room and immediately drift asleep thinking about him.

We don't kiss because we'd never be able to stop.

"Are you going to be okay?" he says, shooting a look at the house.

"Oh, yeah," I say. "Yeah."

He blows me a kiss. I'm so happy-dizzy-shaky, I feel as if I have someone else's head on as I walk up the porch stairs. When I open the door something goes sailing across the room and hits me hard in the temple.

Curtis says, cold and tight: "I didn't mean to hit you, Deirdre."

He picks up the heavy book at my feet and hurls it at a far wall. It bounces off and smashes a vase on the TV.

I'm touching my head where it feels as if it should be bleeding, but nothing wet comes off on my hand. Curtis has never hit me before, but he's thrown books and ashtrays, usually against walls.

He's standing in front of me, his mouth set tight and a vein pulsing in his neck. He's trying to look casual, slouching, with his thumb hooked into his belt loop. As his shoulders rise and fall, he gives a forced snort of laughter. "What were you planning to do with your fists?"

And then I realize my hands are clenched. For once in my life I don't feel like running or cringing in the face of his rage. Without even thinking about it, I'm at his face, my hands flying, wanting to bash his face in, the bastard, hitting me with a book, all those years of trashing Mom, I want to kill him. . . .

But he grabs my wrists and practically throws me onto the couch. He hulks over me. I mash my fists into my eyes.

"That's right," Curtis says. "You should cry."

I try to get up but he puts his hand on my shoulder and pushes me down.

He's got his head tilted to the side, so he has to slide his eyes around to look at me. Mr. Calm. "I can't imagine who you think you're dealing with. Yeah, cry, Dee! It's good for ya. You're the victim here and victims always cry."

He's talking to me just the way he used to talk to my mother when she'd cry because he was hanging out with some new model. He'd turn it around and make it her fault somehow. He'd criticize the way she looked or the way the house looked or sometimes start imitating the way she walked or talked, telling her she was being phony and weird.

I try for tough, but my voice comes out small. "What's this about, Curtis?"

He stands with his head cocked, glaring at me. At first he doesn't answer. Then: "If you're going to act like a slut, if you're going to act like a spoiled-brat slut and you're going to do things your way, hey, kid, there's a payoff."

He probably thinks I slept with Johnny. I don't care what he thinks, I have to get out of there.

"You're crazy." I scramble off the couch.

He leans hard on my shoulder again.

"I don't think so," he says. "I think you're the one who's crazy. Let's take a look at your behavior. You've been spending your time completely self-absorbed, not giving a crap about your brother or your father, and then you go out and screw all night and then come sneaking back into my house."

"I didn't sneak in! I didn't do any of that—and it's none of your sucking business!"

"Don't scream at me, Deirdre," he says. "I'm going to tell you this once. Don't even try raising your voice to me."

"Oh, God," I say, hysterical, snot running down my face, shaking. "What do you want from me?"

"I want you to shut up and listen."

I sit rocking on that couch, my hand on my mouth, weird strangled sounds coming out of my throat.

Now he's kneeling down near me. I want to kick his face in. "Kid, you know that I love you," he says quietly.

"No you don't!" I scream.

"I'm going to ignore that." Same quiet voice. "Check yourself out, Dee. Wow, look at you." He shakes his head in amazement. "You're really out of control. No one got you in this state but you. And you know why? You know why? Because you didn't listen to me."

I wipe my nose on my sleeve. I don't care about anything anymore. I feel as if I've been here before and I'll be here again and I'm never going to get out of this.

"You know what I'm talking about," he says.

"I don't!"

"Stop shrieking at me. I told you . . ." He stops and lets out a sigh as if he's normally a tolerant man but I've used up every last ounce of his patience. "I told you not to see him again until I met him."

He nods. "This is the same guy who left you, left you all desperate and upset. The same cold bastard, am I right, Dee?"

"He's not a cold bastard."

"And then he came looking for you when he was good and horny, am I right, Dee? Is that what happened?"

"Don't talk to me like that," I say.

"Like what?" he says, raising his voice and standing up. "Like a father? About sex? You don't have a mother anymore, so who's supposed to tell you not to act like a slut? Kenny? Yeah, I think that's a good idea. Let's get Kenny down here."

I'm shouting *No!* and he's bellowing *Kenny!* and my heart just folds over, crushed.

I hear Kenny's heavy feet on the stairs. Curtis says: "Come on in, Ken, we're having a little family meeting." Curtis flicks on a lamp and I blink in the light. Inquisition time.

Kenny's face is blotchy and his eyes are dazed. He's been crying. He's almost as tall as Curtis but he's half as skinny, a kid. He looks at me and winces. Don't, I want to tell him. It's okay. We'll get out of this. You don't have to be the one to save me.

Curtis sits down on the floor cross-legged before me, gestures with his hand at the couch. The happy host. "Sit down, Kenny, sit down."

Kenny sits next to me on the couch, stiff, with his hands in his lap.

"We're a happy family, right?"

No answer.

"You take this one, Deirdre. Are we a happy family?"

"No."

"Ah," he says. "And tell me, were we ever a happy family?"

No answer.

He's glaring at me, his eyeballs bloodshot, every muscle in his face tense. "I said, were we ever?"

"Dad . . . ," Kenny says.

"Let her answer," Curtis says, not taking his eyes from my face.

"Yeah, okay," I say. "We were once. Before—"

"Before what? You don't know. You see, you don't know, do you? But *you* know." He snaps his eyes to Kenny. "Why don't you let her in on the secret, Ken?"

Kenny looks at me helplessly, at his hands, at the front door. "Dad, I don't want to do this."

"Come on, Kenster," says Curtis, rising to his feet, voice rising too, as if he's a nasty lawyer in court. "Any possible notions of why we were once a happy family and why we are not a happy family any longer?"

There's something in the way Kenny's holding himself so rigidly, his arms wrapped around himself. He's keeping something in and I know it has to do with whatever happened to change everything years ago.

Curtis is silent, pacing. Then: "Do you remember, Kenny, that afternoon when you came home from baseball practice and your mother was in the kitchen—"

"Stop it!" Kenny yells.

Curtis says, "Actually, I'm not going to stop. Not until you tell Deirdre what happened. I don't want any more secrets in this happy family."

"Leave him alone," I say. My voice is quiet, businesslike, borrowed from Curtis. I sense that for all Curtis's lies and twisted sense of reality, whatever he's going to tell really did happen. And I don't want to hear it.

Curtis kneels in front of Kenny. "Do you remember that afternoon when you got home and your mother was in the kitchen with her tongue down a man's throat? A boy, actually, twenty-five if he was a day. Do you remember? Do you?"

My knees are shaking.

Kenny's so freaked, he's crying without tears.

"And you told me about it, Kenny, right?" Curtis's voice is soft and encouraging.

"I'm sorry," Kenny finally says.

He's weeping, head in his hands. I haven't seen my brother cry since he was a tiny kid. And Kenny must've been eight when he saw Mom with someone. I try to remember seeing some young guy in the house. Mom always had lots of friends. The only face I can come up with was some friend of hers, Bobby. He was so cute, I almost had a crush on him. He was sweet, too, and funny. And then this long-ago memory comes back of Curtis raging about him. Mom screaming, crying. I remember thinking Curtis was making up lies about Bobby. And then Bobby never came anymore.

I never thought of Mom as capable of kissing another man. And Curtis never seemed to care about what Mom did. I thought Mom was the jealous one. It sort of makes sense, though. If Mom were here I'd run to her and hug her. But if she were here she'd already be hugging me. Curtis would never get away with talking to us like this if she were here.

"I guess this puts it all in place for you, Dee, doesn't it?" Curtis says. "Now you have that one missing piece that explains it all, right?"

I can't answer him. I feel as if he's leading me down some tricky path and I'm going to end up in a trap. When I was a little kid and he and Mom would fight, I didn't know whose side to take. Curtis would call her a victim and crazy and weak and he said it so convincingly I thought some of it must've been true. I didn't want to believe that about her, but I didn't want to think my father was crazy either.

I started hating Curtis. It became easy to side with Mom because she was the one who never yelled at me without reason or without apologizing afterward. She was my friend. Most of the time she was happy and if she was sad she didn't take it out on me, just cried quietly in her room.

But every so often now, Curtis says things about me, even twisted things, that seem to have some truth in them. Like maybe Johnny really did find me because he wanted sex. But no, I know it was about love. He never tried to push me into things I didn't want.

Curtis has that way of getting into my mind sometimes.

He's standing over me. "Now you know the one thing, right, Dee? Now you know."

I sense he's about to run out of steam and if I just answer him he'll shut down and let Kenny and me out of this nightmare.

"Yeah, Curtis, now it all makes sense."

"Right?" he says. "Doesn't it? It makes sense that a man would fall apart when his child, his only son, tells him that he saw his mother being a slut. It makes sense, doesn't it?"

"Mom's not a slut," Kenny says through gritted teeth. "She's not." He stands up.

"Let me finish," Curtis says.

"And Dee's not a slut," Kenny says, louder, getting in Curtis's face. And then *wham,* he backhands Curtis in the face, so hard that Curtis staggers backward. Kenny stands there, ready to give more. Curtis is rubbing the side of his jaw, forcing a grin. But then his face crumples.

"Deirdre," he says, as if he hasn't just been hit, as if he doesn't have tears sliding down his face. "Let's establish this fact once more. It makes sense, right?"

"Right." I'll say anything at this point.

"Wrong!" says Curtis, pointing a finger at me like a gun. "Maybe one event got it started, but that's not what it's all about. That's exactly your whole problem. You think everything works in a reasonable manner. But life doesn't work like that. I didn't want to smash your illusions, because you loved her so much, you wanted to believe in her so much. Now I see I have to smash it all for you. You're lucky; usually illusions get dismantled bit by bit over a lifetime—they get wrecked and then you build them up a little and then they get wrecked again. . . ."

Kenny and I glance at each other. Curtis is so gone, pacing and muttering and lost in his own great speech, that we could almost have a conversation and he wouldn't notice. Kenny sits back down on the couch and I am so grateful he's here with me. We have to play this out.

"Maybe one event can turn your life into a toilet," Curtis says, "but that boy in the kitchen was nothing. Deirdre, Kenny . . ." He whirls around and faces us. "Your mother was too damn hopeful, that was the problem. And every time I saw that hopeful face, that butterflies-and-candies-and-flowers face, it was like a slap. I couldn't stand it. It reminded me of everything I couldn't give her." He falls down on his knees, puts his head in his hands. And then, as if the idea has just hit him: "I used to think she was doing it on purpose. Do you know?" he says. "Do you know? Oh, kids, I'm so sorry. I'm so sick; I'm so rotten."

Kenny and I get up and leave him there.

Up in my room I hear Curtis moaning, "Come back, guys. I loved her. We should light candles for her. Pray for her. We need to be a family again. Buy curtains, light candles, be a family . . ."

Long after Curtis has passed out on the couch and his moans give way to snores, I hear Kenny sniffling in his room. I knock softly, open the door.

I sit on his bed. "I want to thank you, Kenny, for smashing Curtis in the face."

Kenny turns his head away from me, shoots a punch straight from the shoulder into the pillows against his headboard. "I can't believe I hit Dad," he says. "God, I can't believe it, Dee."

"It's okay, Kenny." For once I don't mind reassuring him, taking care of him a little. I feel like a normal big sister. I'd pat his back or something, if it wouldn't insult him. "He deserved it, Kenny. I know you love him, but he deserved it."

"It's not that," Kenny says, sitting up, wiping his face on his sleeve. He has a new, wild look in his eyes. "It's that I've wanted to do it for such a long time."

Chapter 11

When I get up the next day, my eyes are so swollen from crying, I look like a Vietnamese girl. Inside I feel tired and kicked and I want to crawl back into my bed and stay there all day. I have little alarms going off inside me, though: Get out, watch out for Curtis. But the house is empty. Kenny is already off to school. Curtis is gone. I have to get moving.

It's warm and blue and springlike outside and there's no sign of Johnny either. I'm sure he's off to New Orleans with Leander. Our kisses seem as if they happened years ago. By the time I pass the park, looking quickly through the front gates for any sign of his dark hair, the flash of the accordion, I actually feel a strange relief about not seeing him. And anger. Where was he when Curtis was torturing me last night? How could he let that happen to me? Even though I know it doesn't make sense, it wasn't his fault. Unless it was.

My face flushes hot and I walk faster, my feet crashing heavy on the pavement, trying to pound the worst thought out of my head: Maybe Curtis was right and Johnny doesn't care about me at all.

As the day passes, nothing matters, not school, or the idea of love. Everything passes through me like noise.

The one thing that comes up sharp in my mind is: I don't want to see Curtis. Walking home, my stomach feels like a fist and I try to prepare myself to see his face, to hear him whistling in the kitchen or see him painting outside with Robyn. I can't think of any way to armor myself. I'm so glad that Kenny'll probably be home. Not just glad, ecstatic. I keep holding that idea in my head: *Kenny'll be there, Kenny'll be there,* as I walk that endless walk back home.

Right before I turn onto Olive, I hear this unearthly sound. It's like a creaky old lady imitating a lamb or something. And there along the side of a mint-green house, tied up, is a bony white goat. She looks at me with round, flat, yellow eyes, the pupils like sharp black lines down the center. She lets out that cry again. The sight of the goat makes me shudder. I flash on the weeks after Mom died when I was so crazy missing her that I imagined her soul was talking to me through Marissa's little cat, through my friend Colette's new puppy, and once, I imagined it through a painting of a woman I saw hanging at the Met.

The first time I did it was right after Mom's memorial ceremony. We were standing outside Curtis's studio, where we'd had the service, waiting for a friend's car to pull up. A flock of pigeons landed at our feet and most of them were gray and white but one was brown and sweet-looking, and I remember thinking—Mom, talk to me, give me a sign, is that you? And then I got a good look at that pigeon's eyes and they were strange and hard like a doll's, as if there was no soul inside, not even a bird soul.

That's how this goat's eyes look. They make me think of the swamp alligators and the hollowness of the world, the coldness. I remember, suddenly, what Johnny told me about love—love like a sword, like an angel, always with you. But there was no love when we were trapped in that room with Curtis last night.

When I get home Curtis is still gone. Kenny's standing in the kitchen reading a note:

Back in a few.

"And he left this," Kenny says, handing over a hundred-dollar bill. Curtis had been flashing around cash the past few days since a few of his paintings sold. He probably took off for a few hours, maybe a few days. We're thrilled.

Curtis would take off after fights with Mom.

142

When he came back she'd be almost glad to see him. He was like another person usually, composed and acting as if he'd never said those horrible things to her. Sometimes I'd hear them talking in soft, polite voices and then they'd seem closer for a while. He was so different that sometimes I'd forgive him myself.

This is the first time he ripped into Kenny and me the way he used to rip into Mom. There's something so typical about this routine, the ranting and screaming and then taking off, that it's almost comforting. I realize some part of me has been waiting for this. Dreading the blowup and feeling relieved about the splitting. Dread, relief, dread, relief. Familiar.

I tiptoe around the house, do my homework in my room, stand in the kitchen eating snacks like a criminal about to get caught. After a while I finally begin to relax into the emptiness and quiet of the afternoon. For now, at least, Curtis is gone.

I fall asleep on my bed and wake up feeling disoriented. It's five o'clock. Blinking, I go out to the porch and Kenny's sitting there in a rocking chair staring into space. Little kids are playing dodgeball at the end of the street, their high voices echoing in the warm air. The sky's soft and blue.

Now that it's a few hours until nightfall, maybe Johnny'll be back and maybe—

No. I feel kind of sick when I think of him. Everything we did the night before is all mixed up with Curtis standing over me and torturing me. Maybe all that closeness with Johnny was false. If we were really connected he would've been there for me somehow, dropped Leander in New Orleans and raced back to me. But Mom was always the one who was there for me when Curtis was abusive. Somehow I'd be betraying her if I ran to Johnny with it. I don't even want to tell Johnny about Curtis. Right this second, I'd rather not see him at all.

All I really, really want to do is rent a video, stay in, eat junk food with Kenny.

So we take our first walk together in Charmette. We go around the other side of the park to the little strip where they have a convenience store. We get milk and a large pizza to go, bags of chips and a half gallon of ice cream, and three videos.

"Can we get this?" Kenny says, waving around his favorite vampire movie. He lets me be in charge of the money, as if I'm the mother. He has this goofy, hopeful look on his face instead of just saying "Get this video." I just love him for being so sweet.

Later, while we're watching the movie and I'm zoning out because I've already seen it three times, and two was too many, I start planning out our life. In case Curtis never comes back. Or if Curtis does come back and tries any of that bullshit on us again.

Either way, Kenny and I could run away. We

could go live at Johnny's place. (Okay, maybe I do want to see him.) And then Kenny could have the couch and I could sleep upstairs with Johnny. Or maybe Curtis will never come back and Kenny and I'll stay right here in the house somehow and take care of ourselves just the way Johnny did when he was little.

Of course, we only have about sixty bucks left from the hundred and neither of us have reputations for doing voodoo. The authorities would probably take us away unless I could hide Kenny at Johnny's and I could get a fake ID and a job. There was a plastic Help Wanted sign in the pizza place and I try to picture loading up those greasy pies into the ovens and making change and pouring Cokes.

Kenny's laughing at the part where one of the young vampires messes up. He's sitting back on the couch with a hand in the bag of chips, his big legs and big feet with his fat-laced sneakers propped up on the couch. He turns to me for a second, mouth open, laughing, eyes wet, an "isn't this great, Deirdre" look in his eyes, and I get stabbed with that old love-hate feeling. As if I'd do anything for my kid brother but might hate him for needing me to do it. And I wonder if that's what Johnny feels for Leander, although I doubt it. It looks as if he only has blind love for him. And besides, Leander's an older brother, an older wacko brother in a dress. I wouldn't even begin to know how to deal with that. Wouldn't trade Kenny in for that, no way, not in a million years.

I crack open another soda, grab the chips from Kenny, try to pick up on the action in the movie. No way. Kenny any day over Leander. I guess this is what they call counting your blessings.

That night, in the hallway, before bed:

"Hey, Kenny."

"Hey, what?"

We can't see each other's faces and it's better that way.

"That thing with Mom. You know, the guy."

Silence.

"It was more than kissing, right?"

"Yeah, Deirdre."

"Okay, I thought so."

"Okay."

"I really miss her."

"Yeah, well."

"All right then, good night."

"Yeah, good night."

The next day after school, Kenny and I make up a real list and walk over to the bigger store on Olive

146

and buy real food—chicken, fruit, stuff like that—
and carry it in four bags with our arms breaking back
to the house. We stop dead on the sidewalk. . . .

He's back.

His van's pulled up in front. Our front door is
open and Curtis's laughter barks out onto the street.

Robyn pokes her head out the front door. She
gives Kenny and me a happy wave. Curtis pops out,
grinning. "Kids," he says. "Kids, what are you doing?" He shakes his head, amused, and scoots down
the steps to grab a bag from each of us. He kicks the
doors of his van shut.

"You bought food with that money?" He's still
shaking his head in wonder. Kenny and I follow him
up into the kitchen. There's no way out of this.

"Are these great kids, or what?" he says to Robyn.
"I leave them a hundred bucks and they get food."

Robyn shrugs. "They had to eat," she says.

"There's food in the house," Curtis says, but
looking a little unsure. He starts patting his pockets,
then hands Kenny and me each a twenty. "I wanted
you to get something for yourself. Go ahead, live a
little."

Kenny mutters thanks. I say nothing.

Curtis eyes me. Steps back toward the pantry at
the far end of the kitchen and beckons me over.

I shoot a look at Kenny. He's hanging back, looking miserable. Curtis beckons again, for Kenny to

come too. Robyn's at the table examining her nails. Curtis grabs me up in a sudden hug. Something caves inside me.

"I'm sorry," he says into my ear. He pulls back, eyes searching mine. Puts his hand on Kenny's shoulder, gives him the same manly "I'm sorry." Kenny flinches. Curtis takes in the flinch with a quick narrowing of his eyes. He says quietly, "Deirdre, I'm really sorry. I was out of hand. We'll talk. It won't happen again. Kenny, man, it won't."

"Okay," Kenny says.

I say nothing.

"It doesn't sound okay," Curtis says, but he's getting that twinkle in his eye. He knows he's forgiven. "You sound pissed."

"I am a little." Kenny looks scared.

"It's okay," Curtis says. "I don't blame you. But get over it, both of you, because"—his voice is all jolly now—"we're having a party, folks!"

For the next forty-eight hours all we hear about is the Party. How the Party is going to bring us closer. How the Party will bring together Kenny's friends, my friends, Curtis's art world, the scholastic world of Charmette High. We'll meet new people, let the neighborhood know we're here, open up the doors and let in some air and life.

It's as if Curtis has turned into some kind of psycho Mr. Rogers.

With all the preparations for the Party—Robyn dealing with Mr. Clean vs. Murphy's Oil Soap for the floors; pink vs. blue crepe paper for the decorations; chicken vs. ribs for the food; Kenny and me endlessly being sent to the stores; washing the windows, fixing up the yard; Curtis overseeing everything as if this is the happiest event of his life—there's hardly time to think about the big questions, like who's Kenny going to invite if he doesn't have any friends? For that matter, who am I going to invite? Is Johnny back yet? And are we all going to pretend the night in the living room didn't happen?

I get Kenny alone the night before the party. I'm coming out of the bathroom, carrying loads of dirty clothes. He's walking in with a stack of freshly washed towels.

"Wait a sec," I say, leaning in the doorway.

He's biting his lip.

"Is this . . ." I'm not even sure what I want to say. "The whole thing with Curtis, you're okay about it now? I mean, I know you're not okay about it, but are you just going to let it go?"

Kenny shifts the weight of the towels. "Deirdre," he says, "he's Dad."

I feel a wave of unreality, trapped here in this bathroom, hands full of laundry, in this moment, in this life. Powerless. It's such a strong flash, as if I stood up too fast and I'm dizzy.

"Are you okay, Dee?"

I manage to nod.

"You look sick or something."

"I'm okay."

He nods. We brush past each other then, each of us diving back into our jobs. The Party must go on.

Chapter 12

By Friday afternoon there's a hot buzz in school about the great event that night, and then and only then do I start feeling as if it's *my* party.

Tanya and Aurora have already gone out and bought new clothes; I know every detail of their mall outfits because it's all they talk about.

First thing in the morning, Tanya's sidling up to me asking me what I bought.

"Nothing."

"Girl, am I going to have to force you to go with me after school to Monica's? It's this little shop near the park. You'll love it. It's so, you know, Yank."

And I know I'll hate it, I know it will be total plastic trash, but suddenly I get a tiny drop of clothes-lust in my blood, that feeling from long ago of wanting to get something new. I've got some money in my wallet, and you never know—Johnny might come back in time and I just might want to see him and it might be good to be wearing something new.

Jane's coming to the party too. Ever since I saw her at the Nubian we say hi and how you doing and what's up. But I jump a little when she comes up to me after first period. I'm shoving stuff in my locker and I drop a few books and bend to pick them up.

Her face is smooth, no forced smile, no smile at all, but no nastiness either. "So, I just want to know what Paul and I should bring," she says. She stoops and hands me one of my books. "I was thinking in terms of food and he was thinking in terms of booze."

"Who's Paul?" I say. I can't picture her with a boyfriend.

"Daddy."

"Your father?" Cool, she calls her father by his first name.

"No, my husband," she says. "Daddy's real name is Paul—but don't you tell anyone." She raises her brows in warning.

"You're married to your father?" I blurt out.

Jane breaks into a sweet, close-mouthed grin. She almost laughs. Gives me a light punch on the shoulder. "Girl, you're in orbit," she says. "Daddy, you know Daddy, he owns the Nubian where your daddy has his paintings." I can tell she's enjoying saying all these *daddy*s, putting an extra bounce and emphasis on the word. "He's not my father. His name is Paul and people just call him Daddy."

"But you married him?"

She nods. "Last summer."

"But you—you're like sixteen, right?"

"Seventeen, uh-huh."

"But if you're married, how come you're going to school?" I slam my locker shut.

"I guess to learn," she says. She's hugging her books to her chest, giving me that raised-brow look, like: Are you about done?

"What about your parents?"

"Look," she says. "Do you want a seafood dish or chicken, or pies for dessert?"

"Yeah, yeah, that sounds great, I mean any of it, whatever you feel like bringing." I never told anyone—let alone a married woman—what they should bring to a party.

Jane gives me a hard look. "You serious about having this party?"

I nod.

"Then you better get a little more clear on your priorities," she says, walking off.

"You could bring some pies," I shout after her.

She turns and honors me with a grin. "Done."

At noon in the halls, various people brush past me in a friendly way, kids who never talk to me. I've got fourteen kids to walk with to lunch, each one hoping to get invited.

In line at the fast-food shack, a pseudopunk girl looks me up and down and then says: "You going to have reefer at the party?"

"I don't know."

"Well, like can we go?" she says.

"I don't know." She's got black streaky makeup ringing her eyes and she looks like a sad raccoon. Then I say, "Sure."

She screams and grabs her friend, who has painted red and blue streaks in her hair and smells like cherry bubble gum. Then she remembers she's supposed to be punk and limits herself to a nod. Curtis said to invite everyone, whole gangs of people.

"And bring some pop!" I tell her.

Tanya pulls me into a booth with Aurora.

"What are you doing, telling them they can come?" And then, imitating my accent, she says: " 'And bring some *pop*.' You want to trash your own party?"

I wave her off. "Don't worry about it," I say. "The more the merrier, y'all."

"Then why don't you invite *them*," Tanya says. Aurora smirks behind her hand. Tanya's giving the eye to Claire Wright and Liz Haddonfield, who are leaning against a plastic partition, sending me big smiles, like my long-lost best friends.

"Oh, please," I say.

It's not trendy. In fact, I found it on a sale rack way in the back, hanging with last year's nylon and vinyl things. It's not something I'd ever wear out to a party in the city because it's not black or tight or even all that sexy. But when I come out of the changing room modeling the white dress—it's made out of some cozy fabric like a sweatshirt and you just slip it on, no buttons or zippers—I feel like never taking it off. Tanya nods, a smile slowly spreading on her face.

"You look like a model," the salesgirl tells me.

What I really look like is me. Not New York me, but the new Southern, swampy, going-to-her-crazy-father's-party me.

The dress reminds me of something Mom might've worn. She was always talking about "quiet chic," clothes that weren't flashy but made you feel like yourself. I have such an urge to have her here again. To let her see me like this.

She loved parties so much, quiet ones, though. I don't know what she would've thought of Curtis's party.

The last party Mom and I talked about was my sweet sixteen. We dreamed up all kinds of scenarios, like having it be a fancy dinner at the Russian Tea Room or renting a place and creating a nightclub for the evening. We didn't have the money for such wild events, but we had fun with our fantasies. Sometimes we talked about what we might really do—a sleepover with my best friends and maybe a show for Marissa and me. I loved talking about the party. But Mom died when I was fifteen and my sixteenth birthday ended up being just another nightmare day in that scuzzy apartment in New Orleans, except for the twenty-dollar bill Curtis had slipped inside a cartoon card.

On the outside the card said, "Wild living slows down the aging process." Inside it said: "No wonder you look so young!" I hated that card so much that just ripping it up wasn't good enough. I set it on fire in an ashtray when Curtis was out and then I flushed the flaming pieces down the toilet. I kept thinking that Curtis was an artist, he could've at least drawn me a card. Kenny gave me a globe that was a rubber bouncing ball. I wasn't thrilled with that either, but I kept it. Still have it in the back of my desk drawer.

Paying for the dress, I imagine Johnny seeing me in it. Then I feel a tug again. Mom won't ever meet Johnny.

* * *

It's almost four when I part from Tanya and half run home with my books and packages. It's only three hours until party time and Curtis is going to kill me for not rushing straight home from school to help get ready.

Shreds and pieces from the night Curtis went crazy have been coming back to me all week. I could push away some of the things, but there was one I couldn't get out of my head.

The image of Mom in the kitchen with some guy. I didn't feel betrayed. Mostly what I feel now is glad for Mom. Like, go, girl. I'm happy she had some love in her life, some passion in the kitchen. Somehow I'm sure she really loved that guy, that she felt as close to him as I felt to Johnny when we were kissing. Like one person.

"There you are, sugar!" says Robyn, in the kitchen, squeezing out pink roses of icing onto a creamy white cake. "You want to hang up some more streamers, doll?"

I don't know how Robyn made that crossover from Curtis's model to girlfriend, but suddenly I'm almost glad. I don't like her, but that absolute, blind, killing hatred I've had for every one of his slags is gone.

She's been a buffer this week. The few times Curtis has blown up, it's been over quick and it was targeted at her. Little put-downs, like why couldn't she tone down her lipstick, it was so loud it was giving him a headache, or couldn't she lay off the dippy endearments.

Hey, at least she doesn't sleep in his bed at night or tell us to call her Auntie Robyn.

I string up the streamers, trying to twist them just right. I spot Kenny out in the backyard with some big kid wearing a baseball cap. They're carrying a picnic table.

"Who's Kenny with?"

"His friend came over to help us get ready." Robyn wipes her hands on a paper towel. "Isn't that sweet?"

"What friend?"

"Oh, I don't know, Davy, Goliath, some name from the Bible." She's rushing to the stove, grabbing a steaming pot of potatoes with pot holders. "Jeremiah, that's it."

She gets some vegetables out of the fridge, asks if I mind chopping up some celery and onions for the potato salad. I'm chopping away, wondering how Kenny managed to hook up with a friend.

Curtis comes in just as I'm mixing in the mayo. He rests a hand on my shoulder and reaches a fork into the bowl. He swallows. "Dynamite stuff, kid."

No attack. I exhale a big breath of relief, which he mistakes for weariness.

"Hey, you've been working so hard, you women," he says. "We're almost there, almost there. You guys are gonna have a blast tonight."

He gives Robyn a big squeeze and a swat on the butt, which makes her yelp with joy. "What else do we need, babe? Didn't you have a list?"

She fishes the list out of an apron pocket and Curtis jams it in his pocket. He snaps his fingers in my direction. "Me and Dee are going to take a ride out, we'll be back in a few."

He gives me a wink.

"Okay, sugar," Robyn says. "But y'all hurry."

In the van, Curtis tells me how great I've been, how proud he is. "You and Kenny have been really, really wonderful. I'm lucky to have you."

I'm looking at him, with his wild hair and sunny smile. Compliments don't drown out the craziness from the other night.

"You're into this party thing, aren't you?" he says, turning from the road to search my face.

"Sure. Maybe not as much as you."

"But you've got buddies coming, right?" He heads out toward the shopping plaza.

"Yeah," I say. "I mean, they're people I know, but—"

Then I spot him. Walking slowly on our side of the street, hat in place, accordion around his shoulder, looking beat. Curtis reads my face. Eases his foot onto the brake and slows the van to a crawl. Johnny's about half a block away, still doesn't see us.

"That's him, isn't it?" Curtis's voice is friendly. But his mouth puckers into a low, tuneless whistle, trying to stay cool.

"Yup."

Curtis parks, lets the car idle. I figure we're just going to sit there in the van, watching Johnny walk by. Curtis leans over me and rolls my window all the way down, sits back in his seat. "You invited him yet?" he says.

"Nah, I haven't seen him." My heart's slamming around in my ears now, not so much because Curtis is about to meet him but just the sight of him. I'm wild inside. When I shout out his name it comes out high and strangled.

Johnny looks up in a panic and then his whole face relaxes. He picks up his pace, smiling, warm, taking in Curtis but looking mostly at me, happy.

"Hey," he says.

"Hey." I sit with my arm hanging out the door window, my fingers drumming against the metal of the car roof, but I want to grab his hand, pull him

160

close. He's got this intensity in his eyes as if he wants to do the same thing. Suddenly he dips down a little and peers inside at Curtis.

"Hello," Johnny says, with just the right tone, a touch of respect, no fear.

"Hey, man, how you doin'?" Curtis is giving Johnny the wary eye. And then Curtis opens his door, steps out, and I'm thinking, *no,* he's going to kill Johnny, but Johnny comes around to Curtis's side and they stand, about the same height, eye-to-eye, and shake hands. Exchange names. Jesus.

"It's about time," Curtis says, and I want to die. *It's about time.* Like, I want to see what kind of bozo's screwing my daughter.

But Johnny's okay. "Yeah, I'm glad to meet you," he says.

"So you coming tonight?" Curtis slides back into the car.

Johnny shoots me a questioning look. "We're having a party at the house," I tell him. "Starts around seven."

"Yeah," Johnny says. "I'll be there."

"I like him," Curtis says finally. We've shopped for a whole vanful of groceries and booze without saying a word about Johnny. "I like your boy."

"You do?" I say.

He gives my shoulder a quick squeeze. "What's not to like?" he says. "He's a little quirky, maybe, but that's okay."

He stops at a light, looks me in the eyes. "Kid, I was out of line the other night. Thanks for loving me anyway."

We don't say anything, just cruise along the main street that runs near the school.

"What happened that night?" I say after a while, not even believing the words are coming out of my mouth. I mean, he just said for the second time, he was sorry, and that's about as good as it gets.

"I don't know," he says. He pulls up to the Home Comfort gas pumps. He exhales noisily. "I'm going through a lot of torment. Rage and . . . Nothing to do with you and Kenny. I mean, everything to do with you guys but . . ." He passes his hands over his eyes. "I loved Destiny, you know. I loved her too."

Part of me is like, yeah, sure you did. But I also see him, half hunched over the wheel, looking at me as if he's suddenly deflated, as if all his energy's been drained out of a little hole.

I don't know this guy at all. Even if he is my father, even if he did spend the other night and half the nights of his life crazy out of his mind, he's human. It makes me feel a little sick inside to see him like that. Vulnerable. All these years it was always two fathers in my mind—the perfect one, Dad, and then the creep, Curtis—one all good and the other all bad, and both of them totally powerful. And now here's this new guy, somewhere in between, a guy who's just trying. This hits me in one second sitting there by the gas pumps. It's almost a relief when someone toots their horn behind us. Curtis and I both jump, and who is it but Liz and Claire in some old red Datsun, impatient to get at the pumps.

Curtis and I jam into action. We slam out of the car and he starts sauntering up to their car and I sense he's about to curse them out. I get an urgent craving for a Kit Kat. I start slinking toward the entrance of Home Comfort and then Curtis says, "Hey, Dee!"

The late-afternoon sun's slanting straight into my eyes, making a halo around Curtis's crazy hair. Liz is cracking gum and leaning out her window, eyes all lit up. "You know these girls, Dee?"

I nod. And then it's all over, he's inviting them to the party.

I just get back in the car and catch that pudgy, pink-faced Claire flashing me a grin in the rearview mirror.

"I can't believe you did that!" We're turning onto our street and I feel like getting out and walking. Back to New York.

Curtis's face is full of color and life again. "What?" he says. "What did I do?"

"You invited them. How could you?"

"Oh, you don't like 'em?"

"Right."

"Well, screw 'em, then," Curtis says. "We just won't let them in."

"I don't want them in the house. I mean it."

Curtis is laughing, shoulders shaking. "I forgot what it was like to be sixteen."

"Oh, right, like you don't have people you wouldn't want coming to the party. Like you don't have enemies."

Curtis gives me a totally innocent face. "Name one," he says. "Really, kid, name one."

I don't say anything.

"You see?" he says. "Everybody loves me."

Chapter 13

By the time Liz and Claire get to the party, there's so much going on I hardly notice them.

I'm in the kitchen, pouring another plastic dipper of punch into my cup. Usually I don't like alcohol, but this is good stuff, bubbly fruit punch with rum and vodka and who knows what else Curtis sloshed in. He said not to let any of the kids drink it, but I don't see anyone guarding the bowl.

Even Kenny's a little drunk. He and his friend have been loping through the crowds, laughing too loud. A little while ago he was sitting on the floor by the kitchen table doing some kind of cat's cradle game with Jeremiah. Twisting their fingers around a dirty piece of string, laughing hysterically, both of them looking like geeks.

There must be a hundred people in the house and spilling out onto the porch and in the backyard, talking loud but mostly drowned out by the music, which is cranked up so high, the windows are rattling. Every time I pass the darkened living room, I see half a dozen people, mostly older, trying to do their old Rolling Stones prances to the new beat.

There're at least twenty kids from school. Some of them are totally nice, stopping me to tell me how great my dress looks, what a cool father I have.

Everybody's got their spot: punks by the stairs, the outside kids on the outside, Triple A kids on the front porch, some of them not even entering the house. Just like at school. And that hits me as sort of hilarious and profound—it's like moving these little communities of bees from place to place and even when you take away their hives, they stick in their own preordained clusters.

Except for Jane. Usually she hangs alone but now she's moving from person to person, sometimes with her arm in Daddy's arm, sometimes not, speaking politely, looking into their eyes, directing them to the food and booze or upstairs bathroom, as if she's the real host. She's wearing her usual black jeans and button-down white shirt, but she has on these earrings that look like jade daggers and she's wearing just a smudge of gray-blue eyeshadow that makes her eyes look smoky and amazing.

I had a great talk with her earlier. We spoke for only a few minutes, but she has such an incredible mind. We were standing upstairs, just before the first big crowd hit the party, and she saw me pull nervously at my dress. I was thinking I was going to see Johnny at any second.

Jane read my feelings and she said, "That's why I always wear the same thing—because the only changes you can ever make are on the inside." And then she flashed a rare smile. "And besides, I'd feel like a giraffe in a dress. I'm not into exposing my knees."

I looked down at my own bony knees and she laughed. "But you go, girl. You know you do." And she gave me a wink and suddenly the dress was fine. The night was okay. And it got even better when I started to drink.

I promised Tanya I'd meet her in the backyard about an hour ago. I press my face against the dark glass of the kitchen window, looking out onto the yard full of people. Aurora's sitting on top of the picnic table, necking with a short, blond kid, Derek.

Tanya and Aurora came with the first crowds, bringing along two guys and half a dozen wine coolers. Aurora already had that smeared lipstick, hickey-on-the-neck look.

I don't see Tanya. Maybe it's been more than an

hour. I've stopped looking at the clock because every time I look I get shocked. Last time I looked it was nine-thirty. It's either moving too fast or too slow.

At first I was hanging inside because I wanted to be here when Johnny showed. When the party started I was expecting him at any second, and then I started to get a little pissed, and for the past hour it's been back and forth. One minute I'm like, Is he here? Is he coming? And the next minute I'm not even thinking about him. Or if I am, he's just some person who happens to pass into my mind, not someone I desperately want to see.

That's the coolest thing about parties, certain rules and feelings and typical responses just fall out the window.

When I pass Curtis—he's one of those dancers in the living room, arms flying, shaking around his skinny hips—everything about that sick night seems understandable. I know it's the alcohol in my brain, but if it's giving me this great new understanding about life, who cares what the source is? They say that alcohol makes you see things in a fog, all warped, but for me it seems to make things sharp and clear. It gives me a whole new perspective about Curtis. Like, yeah, he said some terrible things, did some terrible things, but I don't have to take it all so seriously. So he's not a TV dad. I suddenly understand how nothing's permanent. All the things Curtis said to me and Kenny that night, that was then and this is now, so let it go.

It's almost a miracle the way a party changes things. Here I am just a few feet away from Liz and Claire in my kitchen and none of us are weird about it. I'm like a kind queen who has decided to let the peasants in.

Not that I want to go over and give them big smacking kisses on the cheek, but I don't want to bury them either. I might feel different if they'd brought along a pack of SWAs, but they seem to be alone.

Both Liz and Claire are wearing modified prep—black lace shirts and black lace stockings, Claire with a plaid skirt and Liz with suede shorts. They're worse than fashion victims, more like fashion homicides. And that's what makes them seem so vulnerable at this moment. Almost endearing.

Claire's a little uptight, though, fidgeting, but that doesn't bother me either. I've got this loving perspective big enough for both of us. Claire's pink pout melts away into a happy baby smile when Liz pulls a big bottle of bourbon out of her enormous purse and asks me if we can go up to my room and drink it.

Claire takes another slug from the bottle, slamming it down so hard, her mouth makes a whistling sound as she drinks. She shudders and grins, wipes the mouth of the bottle, and passes it on. There's maybe five girls in my room and the hot glow of bourbon in our guts has spread into the whole room, making us cozy as a family.

"You're all right, ya know," Liz keeps saying to me. She's propped up on my bed with Claire, heads nestled together against the pillows like lovers.

"Yeah, she's okay," says Claire. She waves a finger in my direction, her eyes half-focused. "Yeah, you are okay, dokay."

And then Johnny's standing in my doorway. It takes me a beat or two to register this. I'm just sitting on the floor, my back against the wall, looking at him and he's looking at me. But everyone else's reaction is mega-instant: Claire and Liz let out little gasps and try to sit up straighter on the bed. With all the little squawks and rustles and adjustments, it's as if a fox just entered the henhouse.

Johnny lifts his head a little, blinks. He is so beautiful—wearing a black shirt I've never seen, and his hat is off and his hair looks freshly washed and silky. He's got the accordion hanging from his shoulder. He looks completely under control. But I catch some insecurity in the tilt of his head and a quick shadow in his eyes.

I stagger to my feet. "Hey, Johnny, there you are."

I don't go any closer, suddenly aware of all the

SWAG eyes and the weirdness of having him in my house, seeing me in my room. I'm also pissed about something—what?—then it comes to me. He's late.

He shows up hours late to my party as if he's just a guest and I mean nothing to him. In the back of my mind I was hoping he'd show up early so we could get used to each other again after days apart. We haven't been together since the night we kissed and so much has happened since then. He seems like a stranger. Worse than a stranger, someone who betrayed me by not being there for me when I needed him. Maybe an enemy. I grab the bottle from under the bed and take a swig.

"Want some, Johnny? It's great stuff." He looks so serious and stiff it strikes me as hilarious and I start giggling and then next thing you know I'm hiccuping and that makes me laugh even more because I sound like one of those cartoon drunks.

I lurch toward Johnny with the bottle. He takes a few steps back. "Maybe I should go," he says in this quiet, quiet voice.

With an extreme effort I manage to stop laughing. "Come on, Johnny." I go right up near him, lean on him a little, give him my best pleading eyes. "You just got here. Come on, have a drink. . . ."

I'm a little surprised when he grabs the bottle from me and tips his head back and slams down a huge amount. He doesn't even blink or let out any fiery breath after he's done. The fire's blazing out of his eyes—they're bright as Chinese firecrackers. He pulls me up to him and puts his mouth by my ear and whispers: "You look so beautiful in that dress, Deirdre." His whisper wakes up something inside me. My heart starts pounding.

Then he slings his arm over my shoulder and walks me to the foot of the bed.

"Nice room," he says. I see it through his eyes and I wish I had something of myself on the walls or the shelves. "These your friends?" he says, eyeing Liz and Claire on the bed. They look half scared of him and half amused, giving each other secret, roll-eyed looks.

"Sort of," I say. "Liz, Claire . . ." I sweep my free arm around the room at the other girls. "Everybody, this is Johnny Voodoo."

If I hadn't felt his arm stiffen and his hand dig into my shoulder, I wouldn't have noticed what I'd said. I called him what they call him. Not Johnny. Not Johnny Vouchamps. Voodoo. Shit. But maybe he's just holding me tighter because he feels close.

I grab the hand that's digging into my shoulder. "Hey, Johnny, come on, I want to show you something." A couple of low hoots come from the bed, but I ignore that and drag Johnny out to the hall where we can't be seen. He leans against the wall and takes another drink, doesn't even pass it to me. I have to take it out of his hand. He's looking at me with angry, hurt eyes. I take a few gulps from the bottle.

Look at him, biting my lip, trying to get a smile from him. Nothing.

"So what do you want to show me?" he says.

"This," I say, and then, awkwardly—I've never done anything like this before—I lean up into him, put my face close to his, put my mouth on his. *He's not going to kiss me back.* But then he is and—it's terrible. It's a hard kiss, fast and hard, his tongue jammed in my mouth, and then he pushes me away and turns his head in disgust.

"You raped the mystery," he says.

"What?" I just want to do this over again, make his eyes soft again, get him back to where he was, looking at me with love. "What do you mean?" I put my hand on his arm. "Johnny, don't—"

He pulls his arm away. "Voodoo," he says. "You know all about it, don't you? Those friends of yours, you know those kids, you know about all that Johnny Voodoo shit, you've known all along, haven't you?"

"I . . . Johnny, come on." I touch his hand. He grabs my hand.

"You want to hold hands?" he says. He's holding my hand, swinging our hands together. "You want to hold hands and pretend like it was before, keep pretending there's a mystery when there is none? That's what I liked about you, Deirdre." He drops my hand, lowers his eyes, looking like he might break, might stop this whole thing.

But then his eyes are cold. Distant, even though he's looking dead at me. "I liked your mystery. I liked that you didn't know me. I thought you hadn't heard anything about me. . . ."

"Johnny, I didn't. . . . I mean, I heard stuff, but I didn't listen to it."

"Yeah?" he says. He takes the bottle from me, drinks. "Well, everything you heard was true. I am voodoo. I'm all that voodoo shit you heard about me. I'm not some TV character boy you invented. And you're just like them. . . ." He gestures toward the bedroom with his bottle. "I invented you too."

Seeing him so drunk makes me feel sober. Even though I'm still dizzy from the alcohol and my brain's still going in strange circles, there's a part of me that's clear and straight. I know I can work this out, turn him around if I'm logical enough. Only I can't think of one word to say.

Then Claire's standing there, bending and swaying in my doorway. "Guys," she says, "how about passing back that bottle?"

Johnny turns real slow to look at her. Tips back his head and drinks some more. "Get it if you want it," he says, dangling the bottle. "If you're not afraid of catching something."

Claire slides up next to him, eyes all flirtation, liking the danger of him. I can almost see waves of chemistry coming off her and I'm praying Johnny doesn't feel anything. She takes the bottle, her eyes never leaving his, and without even wiping it, takes a long drink.

She points at his accordion with the bottle. "Are you going to play for us, Johnny?" She says it sweet and wide-eyed, as if she's in total awe of him. Nothing sarcastic.

I can't stand the way she's looking at him, the way he's smiling at her. I grab the bottle from her, feel it rip down my guts.

"Yeah, Johnny," I say. "Why don't you play something for my friends."

He doesn't even look at me. "You want to hear something?" he says to Claire.

"Uh-huh," she says, edging just a little bit closer. "I sure do."

He hooks his thumb under the accordion strap and my heart feels stabbed. God, don't let him play something. If he plays even one note, one note, it'll be worse than if he just walked out and never came back. I already feel that heavy, hopeless sense of betrayal.

"Johnny," I say softly. "Don't."

But he's off where I can't reach him. And he's playing.

As beautiful and sweet and magical as his playing was in the swamp, with every note standing out like a separate angel voice, as pretty as that was, that's how ugly this is. He's making these clashing, blurred sounds, like a giant two-year-old playing, only worse; he knows what he's doing, he knows how to wring the most demented sounds out of the instrument.

The hall's filled up with this ugliness. Claire and Liz are smiling uncomfortably, starting to back into my room. But I'm frozen. And then it gets even worse: He starts singing.

In this voice that starts out high and nasal and dives down into a growl like some possessed being, he's singing about how he once loved a girl until he found out how fake she was, pretending to be a poet when she was just a plastic girl like all the high-school girls, a plastic toy. And then, louder than the confused moans of the accordion and his shouted song, is my voice, screaming at him to get the hell out, get out, get out of my damn house.

I'm crazy, thinking with some animal brain instead of my own, all over him, with only one thought, to rip that thing out of his hands and throw it down the stairs, but I can't get a grip on it and he wrenches himself away from me and then he's out of there, running down my stairs.

I watch his back, I watch him disappear, and even as I'm screaming, still screaming for him to get out, get out, I feel part of my heart going out into the night with him.

Chapter 14

"Everybody gets drunk," Jane tells me the next day. I'm on my knees scrubbing the floor, my head pounding. She's sitting at the kitchen table cool and amused. "It's only trouble when it's a habit."

I stop scrubbing and sit holding my head. "I feel so sick."

"Yeah, baby, it'll do that."

"Jane, he was so mean."

"And you were an angel, right?"

The weirdest thing is I feel nothing for him. I'm not sad.

"I feel dead inside," I tell her.

"And you look like a corpse too."

I take a few weak swipes at the floor. "I was so close with him before."

Jane looks at me hard. "You were real tight with your ma, weren't you?"

I don't say anything.

"And you lost her, baby."

I look away.

"Sometimes, when you're scared, your heart can just crawl up inside itself and hide for a while." She gets down on her knees and takes the rag and starts moving it over the punch stains on the floor. "You've got to put some muscle into it, or there's no point at all."

It's two weeks after the party and I'm lying in our new hammock. It's one of the things Curtis bought after one of his paintings sold. He made a connection at the party, some rich judge who loves Curtis's stuff.

I've been lying in the hammock looking at the sky and wondering why I can't feel anything about Johnny.

Curtis comes over and hands me a lemonade.

"I'll get you a headshrinker if you want," he says.

"Gee, thanks."

"But you don't need one."

"How do you know?"

"Because you're only half as crazy as me and I'm doing fine."

"Curtis—you think Johnny was really okay?"

Curtis gives the hammock a gentle push. "Yeah, he was okay."

"Did you ever just stop liking someone? I mean just wake up and there's nothing?"

"Like when the pain's so bad you can't stand to feel it?" He gives me another push. "Like you love them like crazy, love them, trust them, they're your whole world, and then—*bam*—they go and do something that hurts you so bad that you push it all down and you can't believe how numb you feel? Like you got an ice cube sealed up around your heart? Nah, never experienced it."

"When does it stop?"

He gives the hammock a last push. "Who said it does?"

It's been cold these past few days. Not like the blue-fingered winters in the city, but there's a chill in the wind and a sadness. The sky is always gray.

I'm on the bus to school, a city bus, warm and crowded, interior lights on. A few early-morning drunks are rocking themselves to sleep. The loud kids are in the back. The businesspeople quietly click the keyboards of their portable computers. I don't feel startled by much these days. I'm used to all the black faces and greenery of Charmette now, the slower rhythms.

The engine of the bus roars as we go past the park and what used to be a reflex—pressing my face to the

180

window to look for Johnny—is just a memory. He's never there anymore. Or at least, I never look.

I've seen him four or five times since the party. Weeks ago, before I started taking the bus, he came up to me when I dashed out of the house late for school. He was all sparkly and full of energy, trying to laugh and get me to walk slower. And then he blocked my way and fell to his knees and just begged me to stop being cold. He asked me, with tears in his eyes, to forgive him for the mean things he said at the party. That was the hardest time. Seeing him like that, and feeling nothing. I told him there was nothing to forgive. I said I was sorry about my behavior, that I had been drinking too. But I turned away when he put his face close to mine and tried to kiss me.

He tried to tell me things—that he couldn't drink, that he'd had such a hard time getting Leander back to New Orleans.

I had a brief urge to tell him about that night with Curtis, about my own drinking, how I would never drink again, how sick I was the next day, how blank I felt after that, how damaged. But the urge passed because I didn't see him as a friend anymore. It wasn't just what happened at the party. It was everything that happened after we kissed. Of course he didn't know about Curtis torturing me and Kenny that night, but that's when I started feeling different about him. As if he should've been there for me, somehow. Should've known somehow. Maybe that was unfair, but I didn't even want to be around him. His neediness almost repulsed me.

I just looked at Johnny, there on his knees, and I didn't hate him or love him. I felt a distant sympathy, but I couldn't understand how I had felt so much for this person. I told him I had to go, and I left feeling guilty. I forgot about him by that afternoon and when I remembered him again, as I walked home and passed the spot where he had fallen to his knees, I thought how strange it was that emotions could be so intense and real one moment and the next just gone, the way the sidewalk stood empty now with no trace of a boy on his knees.

There were other times. He always looked sad and serious. If he would just be a little lighter, maybe we could see each other again. Maybe I'd feel something for him. But every time I've seen him, he's had that deep look in his eyes, maybe even the one I used to love, only now it makes me feel sick. He's demanding something from me that I can't give.

I saw him at the Nubian Beat one night. It was just after Christmas and they were having a closing party for Curtis's show, with a few dozen people, cheese and crackers, soft music. I was sitting on the stage with Jane playing chess. We've gotten really good; we play once a week at least. There was a close, family feeling in the place, so everyone noticed when the door opened and Johnny walked in.

I saw Curtis rise from his seat and Robyn pat his hand and pull him back down. I don't know if Curtis would've started a fight with Johnny or greeted him like a buddy, but Robyn leaned into his ear and said something and they both looked at me and went back to chatting at their table.

"Watch out," Jane said to me.

He came right to me, his eyes shy. I didn't feel dread or fear or happiness.

"I saw the posters," he said. "I thought I'd come." Curtis had put up a few posters around town advertising the closing party.

I tried for a light tone of voice. "Well, enjoy the show."

Johnny walked around the place, carefully studying the paintings. I kept playing chess but started losing my strategy. I saw he didn't have his accordion and for just one second I experienced a sharp, sweet memory: that late afternoon in his cabin, with Leander cuddled up to the accordion and the room glowing in the lantern light.

When he was done looking at the paintings, and it

seemed as if he took hours, Johnny took out a pen and wrote something on a cocktail napkin. He gave it to me and left without waiting for me to read it.

Jane gave me a look. "Now, you're going to want to keep that," she said. "You've got to know about the delayed reaction thing."

"What delayed reaction thing?"

"When your heart starts working again, only it's too late, and you've thrown out all the notes and all the clues and the guy's gone too."

"Jane, you're a trip."

I spread out his note.

"Meet me tonight at our spot?" His writing was big and childish. That question mark made me feel something like hatred. He was so hesitant. When we loved each other, when it was real for both of us, he would never have put a question mark.

And that night, when the party was over and I lay in bed, I heard faint, sad music, mournful as a dirge. It came from the woods and I had to close my window and lie there for a long time in the silence before I could sleep.

Liz Haddonfield's party is only a few days away and half the junior class is going.

Everybody is crazy for parties in this school. If you throw a good one you get famous. That simple. And

Liz's party is supposed to be the mother of all parties, with costumes and maybe no parents and drink-slamming contests.

"Come on, Dee, you just have to go." Liz plants herself in front of me after gym. She calls me Dee all the time now. It beats Yankee Voodoo. Claire (whose hair looks like sprouted fungus now that it's growing out), acts as if she wants to call me the old names and do the old games like hide-the-towel while I'm in the shower, but she calls me Dee too.

"You can even bring you-know-who," she says with a flip of her black mane. "I mean, you're welcome to, just as long as he—you know—behaves."

"I don't go with him anymore," I say. That's what they call it here—"go with."

"Then can I ask him?" Claire says. She's half joking, but she's biting her lip. I haven't talked about Johnny to anyone but Jane. I remember the way Claire looked at Johnny in the hall outside my bedroom.

I shrug. "Hey, it's fine with me," I say. And it hits me that it really is.

But when I run into him that Saturday, the day of the party, he tells me the only place he's going is out of town. For good.

"Well, maybe not forever," he says. We're in the

185

park. Finally a blue-and-gold day, no clouds or mud. I'm on the bleachers watching Kenny throw some hoops with Jeremiah, waiting for Curtis to give us all a ride to the mall. When Johnny comes up behind me I almost fall off, yell at him for sneaking up.

"It's hard to leave," he says. He's standing close to me and I'm just a little higher than him. He reaches his hand up, as if to touch my cheek, and I involuntarily jerk my head away. He ducks his head real quick and shoves his hands in his pockets. Steps back. I'm not mad at him—there's just no more chemistry.

"Leander's really bad," he says, lifting his eyes to mine, trying to find some connection. I don't even want to look at him, have to force myself to. He's too open, too vulnerable. "He needs me and . . ." Johnny steps back even more, draws an imaginary line in the grass with the toe of his boot. "And there's nothing keeping me here."

"Okay," I say. And I can't keep the impatience out of my voice. "Okay, then good-bye."

His eyes are desperate, his mouth opens, he raises his hand—like, Why are you doing this? Please stop—then just lets it drop. And I'm so grateful he doesn't say anything or make me talk about it, that I almost like him again.

"I hope things go okay for you," I say. "I mean you and your brother."

He looks at me for a beat. And then: "Look, Deirdre, I just want you to know . . . I just . . . I mean, you can use my place. I'll leave the boat by our spot and you can just use my place whenever you need to."

"Thanks," I say. I know I should feel touched, but I wonder if he's offering me his place as some other way to keep me, to trap me. I wouldn't go there for anything.

"I want you to," he says. "Just remember—it's there. I know you can find it."

I even have this flash that he's not going anywhere, that he just wants to trick me into showing up at his place. Total paranoia, but sometimes even psychos hit at the truth.

"Yeah, okay," I say. "Good-bye, thanks." I feel ridiculous saying good-bye to someone who's not walking away, but maybe the words will make him leave.

He starts to come closer and I'm thinking No, God, go, go, and then he freezes. "I wish . . . ," he says, then wipes at the air as if he's erasing a visible memory. "Okay. Good-bye."

And he turns, walking away fast, the accordion on his shoulder flashing in the cold sunshine as he leaves the park.

Chapter 15

I may be the only person not wearing a costume, and for some reason that's made me the target of every rubber-masked, painted-face ghoul and beast at Liz's party from hell.

I've been trying to make it to the door for at least forty minutes, but I keep getting stopped and spun around, pawed and grabbed by some hot-breathed drunken leopard or clown or vampire. Guys saying, "Baby, I got a little voodoo in my pocket, want to check it out?" And "Yankee, want to blow my horn?"

When you don't drink you can see what it does to other people, how stupid they are and how intelligent they find themselves. If I was stuck there for another second, I'd probably be climbing the walls for a six-pack just so I could talk to them in their own language.

Something's been gnawing at the back of my

mind at this party, something about Johnny. I've been looking at every boy, searching their eyes behind their mask holes, looking at the way they walk, listening to them, finding myself almost hoping one would turn out to be Johnny, that maybe he hadn't gone yet and had shown up here.

I try to tell myself that I don't care, but as the night goes on and so do the noise and the stupidity, it gets clearer and clearer to me. I do care. More than care—it hurts. My throat's choked up and I feel as if I've got to see him and fix everything that's been so weird. Now that he's going, or already gone, I can see clearly. I flash on his hurt face, his pleading face, his love for me, and I'm suddenly awake. There was never anyone like Johnny, or anything like what we had. The guys at this party, half the people at this party—maybe all of them—not one of them understands me. Not one is him. If he walked into the room I'd know him in a second, he'd stand out even if he were dressed like a mummy.

I have to see him.

I make it out the door to Liz's vast, columned porch, harlequins and dragons and princesses leaning on the columns. Aurora and Tanya, dressed as mimes with whiteface and leotards, are nowhere in sight. I came with them but watched the roads as we drove, having some kind of creepy premonition about how this event would end. We're only half a mile or so from my house, and without saying good-bye I hit the road.

"Honey," says a girl's voice. "Dee, Dee, where ya goin'?"

Claire's dressed as a Barbie-doll bride, complete with rhinestone tiara. "I can get you a ride if you gotta go!" She's on the porch, weaving and swaying and smiling a goony grin with a bottle in one hand and a plastic champagne glass in the other. "Just hold up a sec," she says.

She grabs a boy dressed in army fatigues, face smeared with mud, and whispers to him, pushes him in my direction. Another guy, dressed as a ninja with headband and black belt, vaults over the porch rail and follows the army kid.

I'm thinking, no way, no way, I'm not getting into a car with two drunken jerks. But the army kid seems okay, sober and polite. And I've got to get out of there and find Johnny. How weird, I felt nothing, I didn't care, he was on his knees begging me and I felt nothing, saying good-bye to me and nothing, and now—I have to see him immediately. All the feelings I used to have are suddenly awake and screaming.

"I guess I'm the designated driver," the army kid says. "My name's Jared."

His friend looks a little weird with a grin like a certain breed of dog, showing gums and small sharp teeth.

Jared's quiet, following my directions, making the turns, not saying much until we get near the park. And then he abruptly turns onto a side street a block before mine and pulls up before a dark lot. I start to tell him that it's not where I live, but then he turns the engine off and ice runs through my blood. He stares straight ahead, cold as a real soldier.

He grabs my arm. It all happens so fast; he grabs my arm and says, "Don't you want to thank me for the ride?"

I feel as if I might throw up on him.

Keeping a tight grip, he slides his hand down my arm and clamps his fingers around my wrist. "Come on, feel me, baby," he says. He tries to force my hand over to his crotch.

His friend's out on the sidewalk, rocking and laughing, a loud, wet, out-of-control laugh.

I say to Jared, "If you don't take your fucking hand off me I'll have you killed."

"Whoa!" He's laughing, rearing back. "I was just kidding, man. You don't have to get all weighty."

I climb down from his truck, start walking toward the street, where there are lights and traffic.

I keep walking stiff and weird, until Jared's truck takes off with screeching rubber and blasts of his horn. And then I run, my feet beating out Johnny's name on the sidewalk, louder and louder, all the way down my block, until I stop in front of my dark house, gasping for breath.

There is such a thing as being too late.

Chapter 16

Even though all the signs are there, such as the boat in the woods, which would never be on my side if he were home, I can't believe Johnny's gone. I spend days remembering the past, thinking I'm catching glimpses of him kissing someone in the park, walking a dog, buying cigarettes at the Home Comfort store, only of course he doesn't have a dog, doesn't smoke, and the only girl he wanted to kiss, maybe, was me.

Curtis has started a new angel series, angels with modern street children's faces. I watch him painting outside one afternoon when it's not too cold. And I remember what Johnny said about love being like a sword or an angel, always with you. I remember how pissed I was that he wasn't there with me when Curtis was screaming at me, the night Johnny and I kissed. My mother wasn't there, Johnny wasn't there.

I don't care what anyone says, love is not always there. Or it's real hard to remember it is.

And here I am with Curtis. Things have evolved. He is not my mortal enemy. He's a little moody, but happier since Robyn started spending nights. And Robyn makes things easier in some ways, there's less work to do around the house and she and Curtis focus on each other, so there's less heat.

I love my father. I have always loved my father. Sometimes, like now, I can begin to put together the dad from the past and Curtis who lives now. I don't have to hate him or worship him. Sometimes he just makes me laugh the way no one else does.

I'm sitting here bundled in the breeze, watching Curtis paint. It's just so weird how time changes things. Maybe real love *is* always there, it just doesn't respond in an instant time frame, the way you might want it to. It doesn't jump up like a genie when you snap your fingers.

Maybe it's delayed sometimes, coming back to you later. And maybe it carries over from the past, carries over and lasts, like Mom's love for me. And for those hours when Curtis raged at me and I felt no sense of Mom or Johnny, when I felt alone and in a vacuum—maybe you're supposed to look at those

194

hours like seconds, and then love will begin to make sense.

I **did** make it to Johnny's place. At first I was too scared to go. I thought I'd get Curtis to come. He knows I've been missing Johnny. He understands about obsession. I was so crazy I thought maybe I could blindfold Curtis and get him to come, just in case some psycho alligators came along. It's so important that Curtis doesn't know where this place is.

It was freshly swept, the soft floors clean, the smell still strange and smoky. Everything gone but the simple furniture and the ashtray with the bundle of sage. I looked for a note, a sign, something personal. I cried, of course.

I **come** here often now, once a week at least. The first time was the hardest, doing it alone. I knew I had to, even if I ended up drowning or being lost forever. I knew I needed a secret and special place, safe from the horrors that might come up sometime in life. A place where Kenny and I could go if we ever had to. But Kenny's doing better now than I've seen him in years. He laughs loud, cries loud. Has a couple of friends. Still works out and still has a little

195

Southern accent, but he's doing good. Yet you never know, things change suddenly sometimes.

So I come to Johnny's cabin. I wipe the windows with newspaper and vinegar; I pull up the weeds. He has a dark green bench in the garden. There are bright flowers along a broken stone path leading nowhere. It's warm and sweet now in the woods; it's spring. I like to sit by the side of his house on that bench with my face to the sun, listening to the birds. If I stay late, I light a lantern. Mostly to get the practice. Then I blow it out because the oil won't last forever.

Sometimes, sitting in his cabin, climbing up to the loft bed and dreaming out the window, I think of that Puff song. Johnny reminds me of the song because I stopped believing in him and he went away. I try to remember the words he sang to that song, and how the notes sounded, but the harder I try, the more the memory disappears. I try to write it down sometimes, the fragments I remember. I tell myself my life depends on it and I just have to remember the words he sang, but they're gone.

I like to be alone in his cabin, on my good days and my bad. I'm realizing now that there are good days and bad. I have days when I wake up feeling disconnected and unhappy and others when the colors seem fresh in the world and my life feels okay and grounded. Things seem to work on those days.

I hate how my feelings shift without warning, like a virus of the brain, out of control, nothing you can do to keep it feeling good, no way to stop the days when the crazy thoughts crowd in and everything seems off.

But the good days happen more and more. This is how I know: I never used to notice good days. Even when I thought I was in love with Johnny, those were only good moments. The best, the most beautiful, nearly holy—but still just moments.

Taking care of the cabin, the one thing he left behind, I feel sometimes as if I'm caring for him. I know so little about him, but I still knew more about him than he knew about me.

Maybe love isn't in the knowing. Knowing is so complicated and endless and tricky, every person an unfinished story. Johnny came with a whole dark fable, the whole town talking about his past. But those few moments in this cabin, watching him with Leander, or those times in the woods, even the twisted horror of the scene at my party, made me know him more than all the people who'd known him for years.

I knew my mother inside out; I loved her and cared for her. But I never knew about that kiss in the kitchen or the thousand kisses she may have had. I never knew about that, but does that change the love I felt for her, because she wasn't the person I thought I loved? I don't think you have to know every fact and aspect and atom and molecule of someone to love them. You just have to see them, see them in a way that's really them, not just something you're making up. And if they're dead or gone, you just have to keep right on seeing them.

Johnny knew so little about me, but he made me feel beautiful. And he left me this house. I don't think I gave him anything. I don't think I loved him in the real way—the way where you want to give because you want the other person to be happy, not because giving makes you feel happy. I almost loved him, though. I think I could love him now if he came back.

It's a moonless night and I'm lying in bed, missing him with a suddenness I haven't felt in months. It's as if he's near, as if we had just spoken and argued hours before and the feeling of his arms is still fresh with me. As if he is just downstairs on the street, waiting for a sign.

If my life were a Hollywood movie, I would stick my head out my window and put my fingers in my mouth and split the air of the night with that whistle I haven't used since Mom was around and I needed

198

to get her a cab. I'd stab the night air with that whistle and then, quietly at first and then joyous and big, would come the sound of Johnny's accordion.

It's a hot night and sticky, and I just can't get comfortable. I start thinking more about that whistle, how I used to love that whistle. How I couldn't do it in the apartment or on the streets, because people would go crazy. It's so loud, it's painful. Now I just have this terrific urge to do it anyway, to stick my head out this window in the thick air. So I do.

And man, it's loud, and it's black out there and the air is sweet and I can't hear anything. Not even a faint echo of my whistle. There is no sign from the ones I miss. No magical music, no taxicab.

But in my head there's an answer: They may never come back, the one I loved and the one I almost loved, but they'll live forever inside my heart.

About the Author

Dakota Lane grew up in San Francisco, New York City, and Woodstock, New York. She attended San Francisco State University. Her work has appeared in magazines and newspapers, among them *Entertainment Weekly, Interview, The Village Voice,* the *San Francisco Chronicle,* and the *Chicago Tribune.* She has also published short stories in German translation. *Johnny Voodoo* is her first novel. She lives in Woodstock with her two daughters.